Boarlander Bash Bear

Boarlander Bash Bear
ISBN-13: 978-1530969043
ISBN-10: 1530969042
Copyright © 2016, T. S. Joyce
First electronic publication: February 2016

T. S. Joyce
www.tsjoycewrites.wordpress.com

NOTE FROM THE AUTHOR:
This book is a work of fiction. The names, characters, places, and incidents are products of the writer's imagination or have been used fictitiously and are not to be construed as real. Any resemblance to persons, living or dead, actual events, locale or organizations is entirely coincidental. The author does not have any control over and does not assume any responsibility for third-party websites or their content.

Published in the United States of America

First digital publication: February 2016
First print publication: April 2016

Boarlander Bash Bear

(Boarlander Bears, Book 2)

T. S. Joyce

ONE

Sebastian Kane slammed the door to his alpha's jacked-up truck and strode for his trailer.

"Oh, come on, Bash!" Clinton called to him in a baiting voice. "Are you really mad?"

"At you?" Bash muttered, quickening his step. "All the damn time."

"I heard that," Clinton said.

A growl rattled up his throat as Bash tossed a quick glance to the woods behind his home and considered Changing. Clinton had been raggin' on him all day at the jobsite and then the entire drive back down Damon's mountains to Boarland Mobile Park. Usually Bash was more patient, but right now his blood was boiling, his nerves firing, and he was sorely tempted to give his body to the bear. He wished he could bleed Clinton, but

5

Harrison would be disappointed, and he didn't want to upset his alpha, his best friend.

He took the porch stairs two at a time and shoved the stack of tires out of the doorway, which pissed him off even more. The door had rotted right off the hinges, and when Bash had tried to replace it, Clinton had pitched a fit. Harrison had given him permission to put up a door, but he needed to order the materials along with everything else they needed to fix up the trailer park.

Hands shaking in anger, he peeled back his flannel work shirt and chucked his hard hat against the wall, and damn it all, it sunk deep into the cheap, thin wood and sat there, five feet above the floor, taunting him. Too rough. Always too rough.

Clinton was right. He wasn't cut out for a mate. Not a human one like he wanted. He couldn't be gentle enough.

A knock sounded at the door, and he crouched as he turned, a snarl in his throat.

"Whoa, Bash!" Audrey said, her cheeks pale. Sometimes she still thought she was submissive, even though the tiger in her middle was a dominant brawler. "You're upset."

"Am not," he muttered as he stood. This

wasn't like him to have mood swings. He was a happy bear.

"I can tell you are. Clinton?"

Bash dropped his gaze and exposed his neck to his Second, then nodded once. "Sorry."

"For being mad? If I don't get pissed off at Clinton five times before noon, it's a slow day. Ain't no shame in *feeling*, Bash," she said in that thick southern accent of hers. Audrey's soft brown eyes flickered to his bare shoulder, and she frowned.

Self-consciously, he covered the uneven skin with his hand and ducked his gaze. For a second, he thought she would ask him about it, but Audrey was sweet. She understood things the other shifters in his crew didn't. She was...nice.

"I have something that will make you feel better."

"What? A present?" He loved presents.

With a grin, she turned and pulled at the neck of her Moosey's T-shirt. A half-moon of torn skin on her shoulder blade peeked out, and Bash went numb. "Audrey," he whispered as he stumbled toward her. He stretched the collar out of the way, revealing the entire claiming mark. "Are you one of us now, girl? Like, official?"

When she turned, her eyes were rimmed with moisture. Confused, he brushed his finger under the drop that had fallen to her cheek. He stared at it with a frown, then studied her face. "Why are you sad?"

"Not sad, Bash. I'm happy. Harrison claimed me last night, and I never thought I would actually get to be a part of this place." She looked around his shitty old trailer like it was a castle and shrugged her shoulders up to her ears. "But now I am." Sweet Audrey. She'd grown up alone with no other shifters.

"Well, you had all of us from the moment we met you."

"Not Clinton," she said with a single, thick laugh.

"Well, Clinton don't count."

"I already told the boys that I'm claimed, but I wanted to tell you last and alone because I wanted to thank you out of earshot of the others."

"For what?" He liked Audrey a lot, but she was confusing as hell.

"For being the first to accept me. And for making me pizza rolls all the time. And for being a good friend to Harrison, but also to me."

Bash hid his smile by dropping his chin.

She gave pretty compliments. Audrey never swallowed her nice thoughts down like everyone else did. She always gave them freely. Good Second.

Audrey turned at his door and stepped carefully over one of the tires on the front porch. "Oh, before I forget. Kirk wants to talk to you."

"Okay. Audrey?"

"Yeah?" she asked, turning.

Bash pointed to her shoulder where Harrison's claiming mark was covered now. "That was a good present."

She gave him a crooked, emotional smile and said, "You're gonna make a mate really happy someday, Bash."

He huffed a relieved sigh as his bear settled in his middle. Audrey waved and made her way to her Jeep. It was parked in front of 1010 for now, but she would move in with Harrison soon. That scar on her back meant she and Harrison were good as wed. A tiny sliver of pain slid through Bash's chest. He wanted that—a mate to take care of, a bunch of cubs, all of it.

Bash took a quick shower and dressed in his best—a white T-shirt and his favorite pair of holey jeans—to meet up with Kirk. The silverback shifter was the quietest of them all, and Bash wanted to make lots of good impressions so that maybe someday Kirk would consider pledging to the Boarlanders. Harrison needed more good men under him so he could be the alpha Bash knew he was.

He didn't bother replacing his tire-stack door, but instead jogged down his sagging, waterlogged porch stairs and sidled around his dark gray Dodge Ram pickup that sat in his weed-riddled front yard. Everything else in his life was old and dilapidated thanks to Clinton sabotaging any plans to fix it up, but his truck was the one thing he was really proud of. It shone like polished iron in the waning evening light.

He waved to Audrey as she drove out of the park on her way to a late shift at Moosey's Bait and Barbecue, then Bash hopped up onto Kirk's porch and yelped when his work boot went right through one of the planks. "Aw, hell," he muttered, maneuvering his foot out of the hole. He would have to fix that for Kirk later. In fact, he made a mental note to order enough lumber to fix everyone's porches. He would surprise them. He liked giving presents like Audrey did.

Yanking the screen door open, he called

out, "Kirk, cover your dick, I'm coming in!"

Kirk sat at his two-seater kitchen table eating a bowl of cereal. "Hey, man," he said around a bite of generic-brand frosted loops.

"Audrey said you wanted to see me. I broke your porch. I like your trailer. It's clean and has a door."

Kirk's dark eyes crinkled in the corner with his chuckle, and he twitched his chin-length hair out of his face. "I know you're on the hunt for a mate, and I thought it was really cool what you did for Audrey."

Bash frowned and sat on the other seat across from Kirk. "What did I do for Audrey?"

"You took back your challenge for Second when she beat Clinton and let her have it."

"I wasn't doing her any favors. I just didn't want Audrey bleeding me." He probably could've taken Audrey, sure, but she seemed good for the Boarlanders. She would make a good Second. She was smarter than him.

"Mm," Kirk grunted, his eyes narrowed like he didn't believe one lyin' word Bash had said. Clever monkey. "Anyway, I talked to Jake down at Sammy's Bar, and we put together a little something special for you." He pushed a flyer across the table in front of Bash.

Across the top, it read *Meet-A-Mate Bash*.

11

Underneath was a grungy font on a black and white brick background. *The Boarlander's own Bash Bear is on the hunt. Serious potential mates invited. Everyone will be screened at the door. This Wednesday only, top three contenders win free drinks all night. Ladies, come get your man.*

And along the bottom was a website. *bangaboarlander.com/bash.*

"A party for me?" Bash asked as he read over the flyer a second time.

"Yeah, but it doesn't mean you have to pick a mate, Bash. This will just get some serious ladies in front of you. It's important you take your time and let your bear choose, or it won't stick."

Normally, Kirk barely said a word to him. He hardly talked to anyone.

"Why are you doing this for me?" Bash asked, baffled.

Kirk gave him a sad smile. "Because once upon a time, my entire life revolved around keeping someone from finding a mate."

"Kong?"

"Yeah. I see Clinton doing the same thing to you—ribbing you, cock-blocking when you're out with humans, telling you you'll be crap at being a mate. He's wrong, Bash. If you feel ready, and your animal is calling for a claim, then you'll do just fine."

"I'm too rough," Bash said low. "And I'm clumsy, and I don't say smart stuff."

"Then find a lady who likes all that about you."

Bash stared down at the flyer Kirk had gone out of his way to make.

First Audrey's claiming mark and now this?

For the first time in his life, Bash had been given two presents in one day.

TWO

Emerson Elliot squinted at the computer screen, then turned her laptop away from the glare of the direct sunlight streaming through the window of Delilah's. This was her favorite spot to work in Saratoga when she needed to get out of the house and be around people. Working from home had been fun for the first couple of months, but now she got excited about a squirrel eating a nut on her windowsill. She'd named him Ferdinand, and he was now her best friend. Work days at Delilah's around actual people gave her the pretense of a social life.

Too bad butt-faced Fred Lawson had snuck in early and stolen her favorite spot in the back corner where the sunlight didn't blind her. He gave her a sneer when she shot him a glance over her shoulder. Ten years ago, she'd graduated valedictorian in high school, while he'd finished salutatorian and never really gotten over it. Canker sore.

"Hi," she said with a wave for the waitress.

Dana was always super nice, and Emerson pretended they were friends. Good gracious, desperation probably clung to her like a second skin. Dana must've seen that, too, because she gave a tiny, disappointed smile as she meandered over to her table with a pen and pad in hand. Emerson would try not to talk her ear off this time.

Hurriedly, Emerson angled her computer away, then ordered a cup of coffee and the pie of the day. Cherry, her favorite, and she believed in signs, so she was definitely going to get some good news in her email today.

And sure enough, when she clicked on the blinking email icon that told her she had unread messages, there was one from the *Saratoga Hometown News* with a job. She was a freelance copy editor for articles and worked for several different papers. Saratoga was the most consistent with jobs, but it was a small town, and there wasn't enough office space for all the personnel, hence her work-from-home gig.

But when she read the title of the article,

her heart sank to the soles of her shoes.

Shifters: The Biggest Threat to Humanity.

Emerson heaved an internal groan as she read the first paragraph. Bartleby Gordon was up to his usual tricks, trying to turn the town against the shifters who lived in Damon's mountains. She borderline hated him. Partly because his articles were always so presumptuous, self-serving, and self-righteous, but also because she was pro-shifter, and these lunatic rantings were poison.

This was the job, though, and the more she considered it, the more she thought it was good that she was the one editing this article. She always managed to take the sting off his vitriol when she edited for him. Maybe that's why Margee, her boss, floated her these crappy jobs. She was pro-shifter too.

Gritting her teeth, Emerson sucked up her pride and replied to Margee that she would take the assignment, and that the deadline was fine. It was a short one, but okay. She lived in a two-room duplex with nothing to do, the new Thai food restaurant on speed dial, and a plethora of pet plants. No responsibilities other than work. For now.

With a quick glance around, she opened the tab for the upscale sperm donor website. If all went well, she would have more to live and work for soon. Things hadn't worked out like she'd dreamed when she was a kid, but she'd accepted she would just have to make her own destiny and create the family she wanted, with or without a partner.

The bell above the door dinged, but Emerson was too engrossed to pay much attention. She was busy reading the different profiles of the donors. If she didn't put her order in today, Dr. Mallory said she would have to wait another month. And Emerson was so incredibly tired of waiting. She had been ready to be a mom for a long time. All that was left to do now was pick the perfect donor.

"He looks like a serial killer," a man called over the diner.

Emerson shot a glance behind her, and sure enough, the giant of a man at the counter was looking right at her. And holy waffles, it was Sebastian "Bash" Kane.

"Oh, my stars," she whispered, mortified as she slammed her laptop closed.

She watched in utter horror as he meandered toward her with long, powerful strides. His boots clomped loudly on the tile floors, and the coffee in his hand sloshed over the sides of his mug with his movement, but he didn't seem to care. He knew her. Knew her! He'd read her message on bangaboarlander.com, and now he was here to embarrass her.

Hand's shaking, she patted down her hair, but that was pointless because her corkscrew curls were as wild as ever, and now her cheeks felt like she'd splashed them with kerosene and lit a match.

Bash wore a white, V-neck T-shirt that clung to his ripped shoulders and hung perfectly around his tapered waist. His legs flexed against his jeans with the holes placed just right at his knees and on his thighs, and oh Mylanta, she was staring. Purposefully, she jacked her attention up his muscular neck to the designer dark scruff on his jaw, then up to his emerald green eyes. He had a nice smile for a man who was about to put her on blast for that stupid message.

To her shock, he sat heavily in the chair across from her, and she cringed as the legs of the chair screeched across the floor. "Cheers," he said, clinking his mug against hers too hard, spilling the top inch off her own coffee. His hadn't spilled anymore on account half of it was already sitting in the saucer under his mug. He gulped the rest down and said, "Did you see the way his eyes were empty? He ain't a good man for you. You need someone with soft eyes."

Okaaaay. Pursing her lips, Emerson opened her laptop and carefully put in her password. Bash had a point. The blond-haired man in the picture was physically fit, sure, and classically handsome, but his eyes were cold as ice.

The giant across from her pressed his hand to his chest. "I'm Bash Kane."

He was introducing himself? Maybe he hadn't read that mortifying message on the shifter dating site. Maybe he didn't know her at all. "Uh, I'm Emerson Elliot."

"Wow, that's a pretty name," he said, leaning back in his chair. He waved to the waitress. "Hi, Dana."

She gave him a genuine smile, not the put-upon one she'd given Emerson. "Oh hey, Bash. You spending the day in Saratoga?"

"I am. Got a day off from the jobsite, and I'm down for a meeting with the bank. Can I have some loaded cheese fries?" He turned to Emerson. "You like cheese fries, right?"

"Do *I* like them? Yes, but I—"

"Me and Emerson Elliot are gonna split one of your big plates."

19

Was it just her or did Dana look disappointed? "All right. I'll bring them on out when they're ready."

"Thanks, Dana," Bash said brightly.

Was she living in la-la land right now? Emerson looked around, and it seemed the giant bear shifter that had come down from the mountains had captured nearly everyone's attention. Most of all hers since she'd harbored a crush on Bash from afar for nearly two years, and now he was sitting across from her ordering them food like they were longtime friends. This was way better than talking to Ferdinand the squirrel or her potted plants. Or Dana.

"Is that the cherry one?" he asked, pointing to the slice of pie she'd been nibbling slowly on.

"Y-yes. Do you want a bite?"

"Do I ever." He forked half of the slice into his maw and rolled his eyes back in his head. "Oh, my God, I could eat, like, four pies. I'm not kidding. I eat a lot. What's your favorite food?"

"Barbecue?" She didn't know why she'd answered it like a question, so she cleared her throat and said it more strongly. "Barbecue. That's my favorite. You?"

"Everything. If it's edible, it's my favorite.

I'm a logger so I use a lot of calories."

"Oh. Cool." Everything was so surreal right now, from the oversaturated sunlight making his eyes look like two glimmering gemstones, to the way his biceps bulged as he wiped a napkin over his mouth.

"Are you finding an online date?"

"Kind of." Nope, she wasn't about to admit she was looking for a baby daddy.

"Let me see, and I'll help. I'm good with reading people." He tapped his temple. "Good instincts. What are you looking for in a man?"

"Well, I'm not really looking for a man, but more like a…friend." A sperm donor could be her friend, right? She considered Dana to be one of her besties, sooo…

"Okay," Bash mumbled, pulling her laptop around to face him.

She squeaked and clenched her fists, barely able to resist the urge to yank her computer away and bolt.

"I want a nice…friend." Emerson rolled her eyes heavenward and puffed air out of her cheeks. She could not *believe* she was having this conversation with a complete stranger, Bash especially. "Funny would be nice."

Bash looked up from the screen and canted his head. A slow smile crooked his lips.

"What else?"

"Caring and generous."

Bash's smile widened slowly. "What's the most important thing to you?"

"Smart. I want an intelligent man." So that perhaps her baby would have an easier time in school.

Bash's face fell so fast his ears moved. He ripped his solemn gaze away from her and looked back at the computer. Silently, he scrolled and scrolled.

She'd said something wrong, but for the life of her, she couldn't figure out what. Above average intelligence was one of the boxes she'd checked on the questionnaire that would match her with potential candidates.

"Sooo, what are you meeting with the bank for?"

"My financial advisor is there," he murmured in a deep, distracted timbre. "He helps me take care of my crew."

"Oh, are you some kind of financial guru?"

"No. Just a logger. Nothin' more." The last part had been tinged with sadness, though.

"I'm sorry if I said something wrong," she whispered. "I don't get out much and talking to people comes hard to me."

"Why don't you get out?"

"Well, because I work from my duplex. I edit articles for the *Saratoga Hometown News*."

"Oh, you're real smart then." He nodded for a while, then turned the computer toward her. "This one," he said pointing to the screen. "And him and him." Insanely, he'd picked her top three favorites. Bash frowned down at his empty coffee mug and encircled it with his hands. "I should go."

"But..." He couldn't go. She was actually getting to talk to another living being, she was enjoying herself, and he was funny and easy to converse with. Mostly. "Our fries will come out soon, and I can't eat them all by myself."

"You're right." A hint of that heart-stopping smile was back on his lips. "I'll help you. It would be rude not to."

She giggled at the funny way he said things and took a sip of her coffee.

"For real, you don't want a man?"

"That ship has sailed, I'm afraid."

"You like girls?"

She laughed again and crinkled up her nose. "I like men, but they don't seem to like me."

"Horseshit. You're a ten."

Wow. That was a helluva line and one not used on her before. Truth be told, she could stand to lose twenty pounds, had wild hair, her face was on the round-like-the-moon side, and she was too short to be called a beauty by classical standards. Still, she liked the way Bash was looking at her, as though he believed what he said. He was the ten. She was a six and a half. It wasn't low self-esteem that made her think so either. She was content being on the plain end of the spectrum, and she was realistic. Bash was a beautiful, muscled-up bear shifter with a smile that made her want to drop to her knees.

And now, she was staring like a simpleton. Fumbling for a response, she panicked and stammered out, "I m-messaged you once on bangaboarlander.com." She gasped and slapped her hands over her mouth to stop any more stupid words falling from her lips.

Bash's dark eyebrows lifted up, and he opened his mouth to say something, but before he could get anything out, Dana set a giant plate of cheese fries in front of them.

"I made them extra cheesy," Dana said. Shooting Emerson a narrow-eyed glance, she leaned toward Bash and whispered, "Just for you."

A vivid image flashed across Emerson's mind of her pushing Dana's face into the fries and screaming, "We are not pretend friends anymore!" Which was insane because she wasn't a violent person in general. Instead, she choked her coffee mug and gave the clingy server an empty *get-lost* smile.

When Dana walked off, swishing her tail feathers, Bash reached for the fries, but stopped his hand midway.

"What's wrong?" Emerson asked.

With a deep frown marring his perfect face, Bash leaned back in his chair and clamped his hands in his lap. "I don't know. It don't feel right eating anything. Not until you're full. I'll eat them all up, and you won't have enough. Go on. You get your fill first and maybe my..."

"Your what?"

Bash lifted his gaze to her then back to the fries. "Maybe my animal will stop rippin' me up."

"Oh," she said on a breath. She didn't want that at all. Didn't want him to hurt. She didn't understand his instincts, but she wanted to help him, so she forked a mound of fries onto one of the plates Dana had brought and said, "This is more than I have room for. Now you can eat as much as you want."

"Thank you," he murmured, but he was

pressing his hand on his chest now, right over his heart.

"Are you okay? Does your animal hurt you badly?"

"No," he whispered with a slow smile. "Feel this." He reached across the table and grabbed her hand, then pulled her too hard until her palm was pressed against his taut chest.

Oh, my damn, he had a rock-hard-body, and right about now this was like fondling a granite sculpture. But under that taut exterior, Bash's heart was pounding really fast.

"What does that mean?" she asked.

Bash released her hand abruptly and went immediately to eating. "I think it means you should say fuck those boys on the computer and be my friend instead. I ain't smart, but I'll make sure nothin' bad ever happens to you."

What a beautiful promise. Emerson gave him a slow, stunned blink as she sank back into her chair. Years ago, she'd put off her plans for a family for a man who didn't deserve her. For a man who had wasted her time, and she wouldn't do that again. She would order a donor sample and go forward with the hopes that she would get pregnant this month. This was just fate teasing her again. She'd learned a hard lesson before, and she was smart enough not to make the same mistake twice.

Sebastian Kane was nothing more than a speedbump on her road to happiness.

THREE

Flowers were flowers to Bash, but Audrey had given him a very specific list of plants that would do well in his landscaping. Already, he'd built a big, pretty porch off the front of his trailer and scraped the top layer of weeds clean off his lawn with the bobcat. He'd replaced it with sod so fancy he could walk around barefoot without getting any sticker burs stuck in his feet. He was bound and determined to make his home more attractive to a mate looking to raise cubs with him, and the next step on his to-do list was to put in landscaping. "Curb appeal," Audrey had called it.

She was at work, but she'd drawn him a sketch of how to do the flower beds, which basically looked like hieroglyphics to a man who didn't have a creative bone in his body.

28

Bash wiped his forearm over his sweaty brow and stared into the back of his truck. The bed was layered in plants and flowers that apparently did well in direct sunlight and would survive the harsh winters. For Audrey's help, he would fix up Harrison's yard next as a present for her. Clinton could keep his weeds.

Bash had picked up two pink knock-out rose bushes just because they were the color of Emerson's cheeks the other day. Would she like a place like this?

A strange ache unfurled in his chest, and he locked his arms against the lowered tailgate. He thought about her too much, but maybe that's what friends did. Audrey was the only female friend he'd had, and he thought about making her happy a lot, too. Maybe not as much as he thought about Emerson, though.

Bash shook his head hard to dislodge his daydreams about Emerson. Two more days, and he would have some serious potential pairings come in for the Meet-A-Mate Bash. Emerson didn't want a man. She'd said so herself, so maybe if he found a girl who was interested back, his brain wouldn't be so filled up with Emerson.

But...another woman wouldn't be as pretty as Emerson. It wasn't possible. And she wouldn't be as funny, or cute when she laughed. She wouldn't have her pretty, shiny, spiraled black hair or her deep dimples. She wouldn't have gold eyes that crinkled in the corners when he said something that made her laugh. If Emerson hadn't smelled utterly and deliciously human, he would've thought she was a lion shifter with those pretty eyes. And her curves were perfect, like an hourglass or a number eight. He'd had a boner the entire time he'd talked to her at the diner. Usually he would've just announced that out loud and taken the awkwardness out, but she only wanted to be friends, and Audrey had told him last week he needed to stop telling her his dick was bigger than Harrison's. It was true, by at least a centimeter, but maybe girls didn't like knowing that stuff.

He spent three hours making the landscaping on either side of the new front porch look like the scribbles Audrey had drawn, and he was sure to put the pink rose bushes right next to the sides of the porch so he could see them first thing when he left for his shift in the mornings and right when he came home after work every day. Emerson roses.

"Looks good, man," Kirk called. He was

sitting in his yard in a dingy white plastic lawn chair with duct tape on the leg and drinking a beer while he faced the sun setting behind the mountains.

Bash stood back and dusted the mulch from his hands onto his work jeans. With a smile, he took eight giant steps back until he was on the edge of the gravel road. Hooking his hands on his hips, he nodded, impressed with himself. "It looks real good."

"Yeah, you need to get that door fixed, though."

Angling his head, Bash stared thoughtfully at the stack of tires in his doorway. A lady probably wouldn't appreciate having to stack those all the time. "I ordered materials from Kong's sawmill when I was down in Saratoga, but it won't be delivered up here for a few days."

"Thank God," Kirk muttered. "I'm kind of surprised a woman like Audrey moved up to this craphole."

"Me, too," Bash murmured. "Audrey is special, though, and didn't have no expectations. What if I don't find a girl like that?"

"Well, you might not find her right away, but be patient enough, and you'll find the right mate."

"You really believe that?"

Kirk took another swig of his beer and nodded, squinting at the sunset. "I do. You're a good man, Bash. A thoughtful one. I don't necessarily think there will be a mate for all of us at the trailer park, but there will be a good woman for you."

"How do you know that? Do you have dreams like Beaston?"

"Nope. I just have an instinct that tells me you will find someone. Look what you did," Kirk said, pointing the neck of his glass bottle at the landscaping. "You made a right pretty set-up for a woman you don't even know yet. You'll find her, and she'll be lucky to have you."

"Like Kong found Layla?"

Kirk's smile fell from his face, and he stared at the sunset for a long time before he said, "Yeah. Layla is his family group, and you'll find that, too."

"But you're a silverback. He always had you in his family group. He was okay until he found Layla."

"No, Bash, I don't belong in Kong's family group. Two mature silverbacks in one crew? I'm registered to Kong's Lowlanders, but we butt heads too damned much. It was an easy decision to come help the Boarlanders for this logging season. I don't belong anywhere."

"But someday you can find your Layla, and your chest won't hurt anymore. Not like mine does."

Kirk's lips curved up in a smile, just at the very corners, but his eyes still looked sad and empty. "I hope so."

"Well, I have an instinct, too, and it says you will. And I don't want to hear that bullshit about you not belonging anywhere. You belong here well enough."

Silence stretched between them as Kirk stared at him with a frown. Bash couldn't tell what was going on in that head of his, but that was normal. Kirk was smart, and his brain worked faster. He could've been solving some long-ass math problem for all he knew, but then Kirk said, "Maybe I'll put my picture up on bangaboarlander.com."

Bash thought he was serious, but he winked and downed his beer. Funny monkey. But what Kirk said scratched at a memory. Emerson had said she'd sent a message to Bash on bangaboarlander, right before Dana-the-waitress had distracted him away from the conversation with cheese fries.

"Hey, Kirk?"

"Yeah, man?"

"Can I invite whoever I want to my party?"

"It's your bash, Bash. Do what makes you happy."

Emerson made him happy. With a grin, he bolted up the stairs and gladiator-kicked his tires out of the way, then stumbled over them and into the living room. He was a man on a mission now because Emerson had messaged him on bangaboarlander. Him. The prettiest girl he ever saw had found him online. He hadn't looked at the hits on his profile because Willa from the Gray Backs had set up the site as a way to prank Clinton, but now he had a reason to check it out.

His shoes were muddy, but he would clean up the boot prints on his dark laminate wood flooring later. His heartbeat was racing again, just like it had been at the diner. He might not be able to talk about science shit with people, but he understood computers. They made sense, along with numbers, where people confused the toots out of him. It had always been that way. He could focus if he thought about numbers, and he could hack just about anything, which was how he'd taken the bangaboarlander site back from Willa. She still bitched about him stealing her fun, but Harrison had asked him to do it, and Bash would do just about anything for his alpha. Harrison never steered them wrong.

His office took up an entire third of his trailer, but that was necessary since he was in charge of all the Boarlanders' finances. From 401ks to investments, he was proud that he was the go-to guy when it came to money questions. Or he had been until Clinton had chased off most of the damned Boarlanders. Still, as much as Clinton hated him, someday, he would thank Bash because, even though he didn't know it yet, Bash was setting him up for life and an early retirement with the money he took from Clinton's paycheck and invested it each month. He was taking care of Harrison and himself, too, and hopefully someday, Mason and Kirk would trust him enough with their money so he could make sure they were set up.

He bolted past the wall of filing cabinets to the computer desk. The trailer park had gone to shit in the time Clinton had been here, but Bash's office was pristine. It had to be for him to be able to work undistracted in here.

He rolled his chair under the desk, and his fingers flew over the keyboard as he linked up to the bangaboarlander site and logged in, password: badwillawonka.

He groaned as the number of messages his page had received popped up. There were hundreds, and all under fake names.

Wetkitty

Bignips

Lickme

Geez. He squinted as he scrolled down the list. Emerson was a classy lady. She wouldn't be one of the dirty names.

Lookingforlove

There. He poked the message and scrolled real quick to the bottom where she'd signed her name. Sure enough, it was Emerson Elliot.

Dear Sebastian,

Oh, goodness, that sounded formal. Uuuum, I don't think I'm using this website right, and you'll probably never respond with all the pretty women you probably get messages from, but I know you in real life. Or, not know you in an official sense, but I've seen you around town. I live in Saratoga. The first time I saw you was in the library. You were in line in front of me, right after you'd registered with the Boarlanders. You turned around and told me I smelled good and you had a really nice smile, like you meant it. I liked that you gave such a nice compliment so freely. I like to tell people the nice things I think too. You were checking out a book on what women are looking for in a man, and I liked that too. It made me think that you are possibly looking for the same thing that I am. Companionship. So, full disclosure, my cheeks are burning as I write this. I've never done a matchmaking site before. A part of me hopes you see it and respond, but another part of me hopes you'll overlook me and forget the silly girl from Saratoga.

A little bit about me, in case you are interested in getting to know me. I'm twenty-eight years old and edit for the local newspaper, as well as a few others. I'm pro-shifter, but I've never been to a Shifter Night at Sammy's. The bar isn't really my scene, although sometimes I wish I was brave enough to go and just try to talk to you. I went to high school in Saratoga, but went to college out of state. I work from home and have only recently moved back here to be closer to my sister and her family, so I don't know a lot of people yet. Anything else, just ask. I'm an oversharer, probably from hours of talking to my favorite pet plant, Spartacus. Anyway, if you read my message this far, thanks for taking the time to consider me as a match. I would love to do coffee or something, but be warned, I will be really nervous to meet you. You and the crews are celebrities around here, and I've never met anyone famous.

p.s. it took me three days to build up the courage to send this message.

Sincerely,
Emerson Elliot

Below that she'd listed her personal email address and phone number.

Bash read it three times because she wrote real formal, and he was flattered a smart girl like her wanted to have coffee with someone like him. But she'd also sent this before she met him, and Emerson had told him flat out she was looking for a smart man. That's why she wanted to be friends.

As he punched her number into his cell phone, his chest started doing that achy thing again where it was hard to breathe. Reception was patchy in the park, but he had two bars if he didn't roll his computer chair to the right. The phone rang and rang, and then his heart banged against his chest as her recorded voice came on, telling him to leave a message. She had such a pretty tone. Clear and sweet. His dick thumped against the seam of his pants, and he frowned down at his crotch. They were just friends. Friends, friends, friends.

Beeeeep.

"I remember you," Bash rushed out. "You smelled like tulips and vanilla at the library. I don't have a good memory. I should've recognized your scent when I ate fries with you, but I didn't and I'm sorry. I read your message. Ummm. Call me back if you want to." He almost hung up but stopped himself. "Oh, this is Bash. From the Boarlanders. We ate lunch together the other day. I like your hair and the color of your eyes and the way your dimples get really deep when you smile. Okay, bye."

Bash hung up and dropped the phone onto the desk. He should've thought it out more before he left a message. Emerson was a smart girl. He should've put more big words in there. Maybe he should leave her another one. No. Girls didn't like that. The book had told him that much in chapter one before he got bored to shit reading it and returned it to the library. There hadn't been a single picture in it.

He didn't know how long he sat there debating whether he'd done the right thing, but when his cell phone rang, he nearly jumped out of his skin. Fumbling with the phone, he accepted the call and said, "Hello?"

No answer.

"Hello?" he asked again. His chest hurt so damned bad, he doubled over the pain.

"Hi, Bash," Emerson said, so softly he thought he'd imagined it. But then she said, "I got your message."

"I got your message, too. I like what you named your pet plant." Bash frowned and shook his head. "I mean, I have a question. Well, I have lots of questions because I want to know everything about you, but I have a big question I want to ask you. Right now."

Emerson giggled that pretty tinkling sound, like a metal knife on some fancy wine glass. "Okay, shoot."

"Okay." Bash swallowed hard and pulled the folded-up flyer from his back pocket. "There's this party at Sammy's, and I know you said it isn't your scene, but I was wondering if you wanted to go. As friends." The last part was bitter in his mouth, but he was fishing, and a good fisherman was gentle with the lure.

"Oh. Well, what kind of party is it?"

"My friends are throwing it for me, so I can find a mate."

"A mate?" she asked, her voice sparking with shock.

"Yes. I've been ready for one for a long time but girls in the trailer park was against the rules for a long time. My alpha just lifted the rules, so I'm lookin'."

"You want a mate?" she whispered.

"Of course. I want a lady and cubs and a little family to fit in with my big family, the Boarlanders. The party could be fun. Kirk told me the top three contestants that I choose drink for free, and I already pick you, so you wouldn't have to buy a single drink. I know you aren't wanting to be a mate, but we could have some fun. You could help me pick a good girl to take out."

There was something odd in her voice when she asked, "Will you pick a mate that night?"

"No, no. Kirk says I need to take my time. I need someone who eases the hurt in my chest like you do."

Emerson was quiet for a long time, and just as he was about to ask if she was still there, she asked, "What should I wear?"

"Anything. You would look pretty in a T-shirt or a dress or pajamas or naked."

Emerson gave off another soft giggle, and

he sighed and leaned back in his office chair, reveling in the sound of her happiness.

"Okay, I'll go. What time is your party?"

"It's Wednesday at seven o'clock. I can pick you up if you want."

"Oh, Wednesday. Well, I'm on a deadline for work so I might show up a little later. Is that okay?"

Disappointment clogged Bash's throat for a minute, but he couldn't just nod. She wouldn't see it through the phone. He cleared his throat and told her, "Yeah, that'll be fine. I'll put your name on the list at the door, so don't wait in line. Just go straight to the front and tell Ray your name."

"Whoa, like a VIP? That's fancy, Bash."

He switched the phone to his other ear and rocked gently in the chair, his reflection on the computer screen grinning big. He liked the way she said his name. "Yeah, super fancy. Good luck with your deadline. We have deadline numbers here, and they suck to hit."

"Thanks, I need it. This article needs a lot of work."

Her voice had gone all dark and unhappy, and he wondered what it was about, but he didn't know the rule about what was appropriate to ask and what wasn't. He didn't want to scare her off with his bad manners, so instead he said, "I can't wait to see you."

"Me either. I promise I'll help you find a good mate."

The smile fell off his face in the reflection. "You're a good friend. I'll see you on Wednesday."

"Okay. Bye, Bash."

"Bye, Emerson."

He hung up the phone and stared at the screen until the glow went black.

He should feel happy right now after talking to her for so long, but instead, the ache was back.

FOUR

The past two days had gone by at a snail's pace. For one, Bartleby had fought every single attempt of hers to tame down his hate-filled article against shifters, and two, she had counted down each dragging hour until tonight when she would get to see Bash again.

As much as she tried to fight the thought, she had a massive crush on him, but the same thing had happened last time she was this close to her artificial insemination appointment. She'd backed off before, cancelled it for a guy, and he'd been a huge waste of time that spanned two years.

When the nurse at the woman's clinic called her name, Emerson blew out a steadying breath and stood. With a polite smile, she passed the nurse and made her way to room three as instructed. Since she'd been tested and deemed fertile, she'd gotten out of the rigorous medications that would force her ovulation, which was saving her money, but it also meant she had to nail down exactly when her ovulation would happen this month. She'd been peeing on ovulation tester sticks and doing blood work all week, and this morning Dr. Mallory had called her in for a last-minute appointment.

When the stately redhead in the white doctor's coat came in staring at her clipboard, Emerson's pulse kicked up like a racehorse out of the gate.

"Okay, I wanted to bring you in here before the procedure to prep you for what to expect." Dr. Mallory sat in her rolling chair and smiled brightly. "We got confirmation that your sperm sample has been ordered, tested, and is en route here, and from your bloodwork, I think we will be able to inseminate you on Friday."

"Two days," Emerson murmured.

"That's right. Now, we may have to do several before it works, or you could get pregnant this month. I've found no reason why you would have any problems, but sometimes nature, and in this case science, can take more time. Or it could take no time at all."

Emerson huffed a long, shaking breath and clenched the sides of the table to stop her hands from trembling.

Dr. Mallory's thick red brows furrowed. "Emerson, are you still sure you want to do this?"

Well, she'd been one hundred percent sure before Bash had shared his cheese fries, but now she was about eighty percent sure. "Can I ask you a theoretical question?"

"Sure. Ask me anything."

"If I had a friend, and this friend met a man who was excited to be a parent, and that theoretical man happened to be a shifter...what would the protocol be for asking him to be a donor?"

Dr. Mallory straightened up as her blue eyes went round. With a quick glance at the door, she rolled closer to Emerson and lowered her voice to a whisper. "There would be no protocol because it's not legal for me or any other medical professional to collect or administer donor sperm from a shifter. And this question needs to stay in this office."

Shocked, Emerson asked, "Why?"

"It's not my place to speak about this."

"But...you're my doctor."

"Emerson, I'm going to tell you this once,

and then you need to put this idea out of your mind. Riley of the Ashe Crew gave Diem and Bruiser a surrogate baby years ago, and it attracted the wrong kind of attention."

"What kind of wrong attention?"

Dr. Mallory dipped her voice to barely audible. "Not everyone is pro-shifter, and Riley, a human surrogate, produced a dragon. A *dragon*, Emerson. It's not legal for humans to make those kinds of medical interventions anymore. They have to breed on their own."

"But—"

"Emerson," Dr. Mallory gritted out. "If you have further questions about what is going on between the government and shifters, ask Diem and Bruiser. Or ask Cora Keller of the Breck Crew. Ask *shifters*. The government could shut down my clinic and ruin me for life in an instant if they even knew I was discussing this with you."

"Okay, okay," she said soothingly. "I'm sorry I asked. I don't want to get you into trouble."

"Great," Dr. Mallory said, looking flushed and panicked. "Then we'll do everything as planned on Friday, and you'll be better off with a normal human baby."

Normal human baby. But Bash was

normal, even if he wasn't entirely human. He was nice and considerate, and he made her heart beat faster and butterflies flap around her insides. He wanted children...er...cubs.

And now her eighty percent sure was down to sixty-five percent sure she wanted to go through with this. Everything was so confusing, especially with the baffling information dump Dr. Mallory had given her.

Emerson walked out of that clinic like a zombie in slow motion, stumbling over the carpet, completely distracted.

Something was going on behind the scenes that she and the public had no clue about. Maybe the shifters didn't even know. *They have to breed on their own.* Shifters were people, too, not just animals. And what if a pair of them had fertility problems? They weren't allowed medical intervention? That didn't seem right, or ethical. Sure, she'd seen anti-shifter propaganda on the rise after the discovery of dragon shifters, but that was just people reacting to their fear of the unknown. But with this new information, it was clear it wasn't just civilians who were fearful.

The government was on the defense from shifters reproducing too fast.

Emerson drove home in a daze, waving

distractedly to every car she passed because that's what everyone did in a small town. She still had a final round of edits to do on Bartleby's stupid article before Bash's party tonight, and she definitely needed some time to process her feelings on everything that was happening. Two more days until insemination would've been exciting a few weeks ago, but now she felt like she was walking slowly toward a frigid river without the ability to stop her legs from forward movement. She still wanted a baby more than anything, but now having the father be some stranger felt a lot scarier than it did before. If she did this, there would be no chance for her and Bash to have any kind of relationship. But if she didn't, she was right back where she'd been for the last decade, searching for a partner to build a family with, and hoping it happened soon.

At the duplex she lived in, she pulled into the drive and hefted her purse to the front door. A giant Moosey's Bait and Barbecue Styrofoam cooler sat on the welcome mat, and with a frown, she lifted the lid. There were dry ice packs around the edges, and in the center was nestled frozen packages of short ribs, burnt ends, brisket, and jalapeno sausage with directions on how to heat up everything.

There was even a container of creamed corn and a jar of Moosey's World Famous BBQ Sauce.

With a baffled grin, Emerson pulled out a folded note that had been taped to the side.

Emerson,
One of my friends told me ladies like when men send them flowers, but I spent way too much time trying to figure out what kind you liked, so I got you meat instead.
See you tonight.
Bash

Well, that man knew just how to lift her mood. Her melancholy thoughts puffed away like dandelion seeds on the breeze. This was way better than flowers.

With a big old grin on her face, Emerson dragged the heavy cooler inside.

And now her sixty-five was down to fifty percent.

FIVE

No matter how many times she patted her hair down, Emerson wasn't going to tame her locks. Giving up, she clapped the mirror on her visor closed and shimmied out onto the curb of the main drag of Saratoga. She'd tried to find a spot in the parking lot of Sammy's Bar, but the closest she could get was two blocks away.

She straightened her cherry red eyelet sundress and pulled her dark-wash jean jacket over her shoulders, then made her way down the sidewalk, her glossy black heals clopping with each step. She'd bought this outfit from the boutique just for tonight and felt like a million bucks. Or at least she did until she saw the line outside of Sammy's had snaked around two sides of the building. All these women were here to seduce Bash.

Her gaze bumped and bounced from one beautiful, made-up woman to another until she was drowning in a sea of hair spray and sex-appeal.

What was she doing here?

No less than three women pitched a fit as she made her way past the line and to the front entrance where a bouncer, Ray, held the Bash Babes at bay.

"No cuts, beautiful," the bald, muscle-man said without looking at her.

"Uhhh, Bash said I'm on the list."

"Emerson Elliot?"

"Y-yes. That's me." She handed him her ID before he asked for it.

Once he checked her name, he grinned and turned his clipboard around. It was just a piece of computer paper with her name written across it and nothing else. "The list is short tonight." Ray twitched his head toward the door. "Go on inside."

Flattered to her teats, Emerson mumbled her thanks and made her way into the bar.

This was her first time in Sammy's, and it was a lot different than she'd imagined. The lights were dim and hanging from exposed, dark wooden rafters, and every square inch of floor was covered in mismatched tables and shifter groupies.

A tiny woman with straight, dyed-red hair popped her head in front of Emerson's face. "I've been waiting for you."

Startled, Emerson jumped and squeaked, but a bevy of beauties currently leaving the bar looking angry stopped her escape.

The redhead cackled and handed her a shot glass of something that smelled strongly of poison. Whiskey, she'd guess.

"I'm Willa. Bash told me to bring you straight back 'cause the bar skanks won't let him move." Willa threw her head back, gulping her own shot of what looked like orange juice. "I'm on juice shots tonight because I'm currently trying to get knocked up by that burly beefcake in the corner." Willa pointed to a group of sexy giants gathered beside the stage. "You know, I don't think Kirk and Jake planned this out very well because we can barely move in here and everyone reeks of pheromones." She jammed her hand forward. Her nails were painted black with little pink slivers on them. "Worms. Red wigglers, specifically. I like your nails, too. Red like the sex-pot you are, raar." Willa clawed her hands and winked behind her thick glasses. "Down that shot, girl. You'll be holding court at the bar with Bash, and the ladies in here are territorial."

"Oh, okay," Emerson said uncertainly. Was she allowed to drink? Dr. Mallory hadn't told her not to, and she still had two days until insemination. She supposed this was her last hurrah, which left her a little breathless to think about.

"Bottoms up, beautiful," Willa said, pushing Emerson's shot glass toward her lips.

Well, okay then. Emerson gulped the burning liquor and yelped when Willa grabbed her hand and yanked her forward, maneuvering the crowd like a pro. The music was loud, but really good. The Beck Brothers of the Ashe Crew, Brighton and Denison, were rocking out on stage, and Willa lifted her empty shot glass in a silent cheers to them.

Brighton grinned and jerked his chin in a greeting as he played a solo on his guitar. Emerson had heard they were good, but now she realized she'd truly been missing out by avoiding Sammy's.

On the way to the bar, she was nearly squished to oblivion as she played the ball in a perfumed pinball machine of women.

Bash stood a head taller than everyone around him, and as Willa told her, "I'm going to get you another shot," Emerson came to a stop just to take him in.

Women swarmed around him like bees on a hive, but he couldn't look less interested if he tried. He wore a slight frown in his dark eyebrows, and his eyes had lightened from forest green to a blazing lime green that made her heart stutter in her chest. His jet-black hair was messy on top, and his facial scruff trimmed short. His gray T-shirt was tight through the chest and shoulders, and there was a dark spot across the front, as though someone had spilled on him. He leaned forward to listen to one of the ladies beside him, but when she yelled something against his ear, he winced like it hurt and clenched his jaw so hard a muscle twitched there.

She'd never seen a more stunning man in her life.

"Bash," she said at normal volume, just to experiment.

Bash's gaze collided with hers instantly, and his lips transformed into a breathtaking smile.

"'Scuse me, ladies," he murmured as he detached from three sets of claws and made his way to her.

Emerson's heart drummed hard enough to

rattle her chest as he approached.

"Hey," she said when he squared up to her.

His hands slid onto her waist, and he pulled her in for a hug. "Damn, it's good to see you."

She closed her eyes and hugged his neck. "You, too." She meant that with her whole heart. "Thank you for the barbecue."

He eased back, blazing eyes eager. "Did you like the present?"

"I freaking loved it! So, I was thinking—"

"Time's up," a brunette in bright red lipstick announced, pulling on Bash's arm.

He gritted his teeth and let off a low growl. The woman must not have noticed because she kept tugging at his bicep, but Emerson was close enough to feel the vibration on the air. She rested her hand on his chest, and the sound settled. "It's okay. This is what you're here for. I'll ask you my question later."

Bash pulled his arm out of the woman's grasp and cupped the back of Emerson's neck. For a brilliant, heart-pounding moment, she thought he was going to kiss her, but he lowered his lips beside her ear instead. "This isn't like I thought it would be."

"What do you mean?" she asked breathlessly.

His chest heaved under her palms. "I thought I would be happier on the hunt, but I just want to hang out with you." His lips brushed her ear, and she went weak against him, leaning heavily. "Layla, I choose her," he said to the blond bartender trying to keep up with everyone's drink orders.

"Finally," Layla called with a wink. "Anyone else?"

"Me!" several woman around them said, raising their hands.

"Just her," Bash said with a hard look for the brunette pawing at his arm again. He swung his gaze back to Emerson. "Ask me quick."

"Oh! Uh, I was wondering if maybe after this you wanted to come over and have some of the barbecue you got me."

His face went completely slack so she backpedaled. "If not, it's no big deal."

"No, no! I want that," he said as he was dragged away. "It's a date. A friend-date. Willa," he called across the bar. He twitched his head toward Emerson.

"I'm on it!" Willa yelled, and when Emerson looked up, the tiny red-head was crawling down the bar top on her hands and knees, pushing two sloshing shot glasses

57

across the shiny surface in front of her. She was getting nowhere fast.

With a laugh, Emerson waved to Bash, then snaked her way through the crowd toward the bar to make Willa's apparent job as bodyguard a little easier.

"Oh, my God," Willa groaned as Emerson reached her. "This is crazy. Who knew dangling a set of bear balls in front of the groupies would result in pussypalooza. Look at these crazies." Willa leaned back on the bar top, her legs folded under her as she looked exhausted and downed another shot of orange juice. "No offense."

Emerson snorted, took the offered shot of whiskey out of her hand, and downed it. "None taken. This is my first time here, and I just came because Bash invited me."

"Yeah, come on bear-tamer. Bash said you're some kind of recluse and in need of friends." When Willa slid off the counter, her black miniskirt hiked up, exposing some purple striped cotton panties. She didn't look embarrassed, though. Instead she gave a statuesque, sandy-haired man up near the stage a wink as she straightened her skirt back into place and murmured, "The trick to getting a hot man to bone you is granny panties and glasses."

Okay then.

Following along closely, she nearly bumped into the back of Willa when she stopped in front of a pair of oversize tables with a group of people sitting around them. The speaker was turned off on this side of the stage, so it was quieter here, and one by one, Willa introduced Emerson to her Gray Back Crew. Emerson shook all their hands and committed their names to memory. Creed, Gia, Jason, Georgia, Matt, and some of the bears were back at the Grayland Mobile Park. Damon and Clara had a kiddo with a bedtime, and Beaston and Aviana were due any day now. Willa leaned closer and called over the music, "You'll have to meet Bash's Boarlanders later. Clinton pitched a huge fit when he found out about this, and he and Harrison bled the shit out of each other, so Audrey is back at the trailer park cleaning up the mess, and Mason and Kirk are in no-man's land." Willa pointed her wormy nails to where Bash was talking to a couple of titans with solemn looks on their faces. "They're trying to keep order so Bash can meet everyone, but I'm calling it now. There is no way he will meet everyone tonight."

"Yeah, the line is almost all the way around the building," Emerson said. "I feel bad, though. Bash asked me to help him pick some good potentials."

"Ha! Bash isn't picking anyone but you tonight. Look at him." Willa jerked her chin toward the bar.

Sure enough, Bash's eyes were on Emerson. She answered his smile with one of her own and pointed to the hallway with the restroom sign over it.

Yes, he mouthed with a nod.

"Go get your man!" Willa whooped with a sound smack on Emerson's ass.

"Anyone need another drink?" Emerson asked, happy to be talking with actual people instead of pretend friends.

"Tell Layla and Kong we'll take another round when they get the chance. We'd sure appreciate it," the dark-haired alpha of the Gray Backs said as he hugged his mate, Gia, tighter on his lap.

"Sure. I'll be back!"

It wasn't so crowded here near the stage, but the closer she got to the bar, the more congested it was with women desperate to get their two minutes with Bash.

When she reached the end of the bar top,

Layla set another shot in front of her and winked. "For the chosen one."

"Thank you!" Emerson called over the country song the Beck Brothers were playing. "The Gray Backs are ready for another round when you get a minute."

"Yep, I'll get on it. Thanks, girl."

"Emerson," she introduced herself, offering her hand for a shake.

"Layla. That big gorilla over there is Kong."

"Your mate?"

"That's right!" She wiped down the bar with a quick swipe of a damp rag and gave Emerson a little wave before she went back to work.

The third shot of the night downed, she hissed at the burn in her throat and made her way carefully through the crowd to the hallway just as Bash announced, "I have to take a leak!"

She giggled at the funny way he said things. Damn, she really liked him, and now he was shunning all those pretty ladies to come spend a stolen moment with her in the hallway. Or at least she'd thought that was the plan until Bash came charging at her from the bar and ushered her into an office. He shut the door behind him and locked it, then pressed his forehead against the door and sighed. "This was a bad idea. How early do you think I can get out of this?"

"Bash! You're supposed to be looking for your happily ever after." Why was she encouraging this? She got green with jealousy every time she saw a woman paw at him.

He turned and crossed his arms, leaned back on the door. "My happily ever after don't feel like it's in that bar."

"You're the one who wants a mate," she murmured, pressing her shoulder blades against the wall next to him.

"But you don't." It was a statement, not a question.

"I did before. I really, really wanted a partner, but it didn't work out the way I planned. Some people don't find their other half."

"You ain't dead, woman."

"Bash...I have to tell you something."

A knock sounded on the door, and a woman said in a whiney voice, "Baaaaaash. Come out and play."

Bash threw the door a dirty look and then pulled Emerson between his splayed legs so close to him she could feel his warmth soaking into her skin.

"You look hot as fuck. And I know I shouldn't say that stuff because Audrey says real ladies don't like being talked to like that, but it's the truth. I like your dress." He fingered the tiny gold medallion necklace with her initials engraved on it—a gift from her sister for her last birthday. His finger brushed her skin, right above her breasts, and his eyes were locked on her collar bones. Bash's intense attention dumped warmth between her legs.

"I like that compliment," she admitted breathily. "I think you look hot as fuck, too."

His gaze lifted to hers, and for a few moments, they stayed just like that, searching each other's eyes, locked in that moment right before something big happens to change the foundation of a relationship.

He looked at her lips and leaned forward slowly, giving her plenty time to bolt. And with anyone else, she would have, but this was Bash. The man she'd had a crush on from afar for a long time, the man who'd fallen head over heels for at the diner, the man who'd won her heart completely with his thoughtful barbecue present.

"Bash!" the woman yelled, banging on the door.

When Bash growled, Emerson couldn't help herself. She lifted up on the balls of her feet and pressed her lips against his. He inhaled deeply and pulled her hand against his heart, pounding like a drum. When her palm was secure on his hard pec, he brushed his fingertips across her cheek, pushing her curls back. He angled his head the other way and straightened up, walked her backward as he gripped the back of her neck.

"I'm rough," he said between soft kisses. "Too rough. You tell me when I hurt you. I don't want that."

Her legs were locking and knocking uncontrollably now as he backed her toward a desk. "You're doing good," she murmured against his lips. So good.

She'd been tipsy before thanks to the whiskey, but now she was utterly lost in this moment. Gripping his wrists to keep her balance, she parted her lips, and he slipped his tongue inside of her mouth. Something nagged at her as her butt hit the edge of the desk. She was supposed to tell him something. *No! Enjoy the moment.* The door was banging under multiple fists now. *Tell him!* His tongue touched hers again, and she melted completely against him. *He deserves to know!*

Guilt flooded her, and Emerson eased back, eyes closed, and rested her forehead on his.

"What's wrong?" he asked. "You smell sad. I don't want you sad."

"I have to tell you something big, Bash."

"Tell me. Tell me anything." His voice was tainted with worry now.

Dipping her voice to a whisper, she said, "I'm going to have a baby."

He eased back and cupped her cheeks. "Woman, I don't know much about much, but I know we ain't done enough to put a baby in you yet."

"No, no, not your baby. I'm going to have someone else's baby."

Bash released her so fast she almost fell forward. He backed up a few steps, and his eyes looked so wary. "You cheating with me? You have a boyfriend? A husband?"

"No, it's nothing like that."

"But you're pregnant?"

"Not yet, but I want to be."

"I don't understand, Emerson. I don't understand." Bash scrubbed his hand down his face and looked panicked as he backed himself against the door across the room from her.

"I'm going to go to the doctor and kind of...get a baby put in me so I can be a mother. It's what I want more than anything."

"But that's what I want too. I want cubs." He wasn't looking at her anymore, but instead his gaze was on her heels, and he was angling his head, exposing his neck.

"Bash, I like you so much, but this was already something I had in the works before I met you."

"But it's different now, right? I could give you babies if you want them."

"Oh, Bash, that is a beautiful offer, but I..." She sighed and looked at the ceiling, searching for inspiration to somehow explain this in a way that wouldn't hurt him. "I talked to my doctor about a shifter being a donor, but she said we aren't allowed."

"I can't be a dad?"

"You can. You can be a dad the natural way when you pick your mate and you're sure about her."

"When I'm sure about *her*. Emerson, I like *you*. My chest don't hurt when I'm with you."

Her eyes prickled with tears, and her face crumpled because she didn't know if she was doing the right thing anymore. "Those men on the computer were sperm donors."

He reared back like he'd been slapped by her hand. "I helped you pick a daddy, didn't I?"

Her throat closed around the answer, so she nodded instead. "I'm going in at noon on Friday, and hopefully I'll get pregnant. I'll finally get a baby of my own. It has nothing to do with my feelings for you."

Bash shook his head back and forth, back and forth. His hand rested on his stomach like he felt sick, and with one last look, he opened the door. Before he left, he turned and locked his eyes on hers. "I wish I was smarter so you would pick me."

He disappeared through the door, and she doubled over her sob. Ridiculous man, he was so smart, so sweet, so perfect. Their timing had just been bad. If she didn't do this, she was making the same mistake she had with Brian. She was giving another man power to postpone her bone-deep need to build a family. Sure, Bash thought he wanted a baby, but he was hunting for a mate, and if she wasn't it, she could be back in this same position, full of regret and childless, in another two years...or even five or ten years.

At some point she had to go and get her happiness, and for her, having a child was the joy she'd waited so long for.

So why then did it feel like her happiness had just walked out that door?

SIX

"You look like hell, man," Harrison said over the noise of his idling chainsaw.

Bash cocked his eyebrows and looked pointedly at the long healing claw marks down the side of Harrison's neck. His skin was splotched with purple bruising thanks to Clinton nicking an artery and causing massive damage. "*You* look like hell, Boss Bear."

Harrison made a ticking sound and propped his foot on the log he'd just felled, then looked down the mountain at the evergreen valley below. "Clinton will fight you pairing up."

"I can hear you, fuck-brains," Clinton yelled.

"Flip me off one more time..." Bash dared him in a voice not even he recognized.

Clinton froze before retracting his stupid

finger to his palm, then ripped his chainsaw cord and went back to work. Good call because, today, Bash's normally playful bear wanted to kill everything.

"Talk to me," Harrison said, cutting the motor of his chainsaw and sitting on a log.

Bash watched Kirk and Mason working below for a minute. They'd both been quick learners, and he and Harrison didn't have to worry about them getting hurt as much anymore. Harrison patted the log. "Come on, Bash Bear."

"Did talking help you?"

Harrison pulled his sunglasses off and hooked them onto the stretched collar of his damp, white T-shirt. He readjusted his hard hat, then gave Bash an icy blue look. "What do you mean?"

"Audrey knows everything about you."

Harrison nodded. "A mate deserves to know everything. Even the bad parts."

"She knows how your dad was, and how your bear don't feel safe."

Harrison's eyes had gone hollow, but he nodded again.

"But you still patrol the border of our territory."

"And I always will, because it's a part of

me. My bear thinks he's keeping you and the boys safe by making sure our woods are quiet. But talking to Audrey, and sharing that burden with someone else, makes it to where I can patrol less. I sleep like a log beside her now where I used to get up fifteen times a night. I ain't sayin' talking about what hurts fixes everything, but it can help."

"My chest hurts. I feel like I can't breathe."

"I can tell, man. You've been struggling for breath all day and wincing your face up where I've never seen anything but a smile. What happened last night?"

Bash stepped over the log and sat heavily next to his alpha. Resting his elbows on his knees, he said, "I think I picked a girl, but she don't want me back."

"Did she say that?"

Bash sighed and watched a pair of hawks flying across the sky. "I don't know. I think so."

"Well, women can be confusing."

"Women will be the damned downfall of our trailer park!" Clinton called out un-helpfully.

"Shut up, Clinton," Bash, Harrison, Mason, and Kirk all yelled at once.

"Tell me what she said," Harrison said with a lingering dirty look for Clinton.

"We were kissing, and she seemed into it, but then she said she was gonna have a baby with another man. A man she picked on a website."

"She's pregnant?"

"Not yet. She's going to the doctor tomorrow at noon. I spent half the night researching on the Internet what she was talking about. She picked a donor because she don't like the stock she's met here in Saratoga." Bash ghosted a glance to his alpha, then back to his boots as his cheeks heated with shame. "She don't want my cubs. She wants to mother a stranger's get."

"Oh, shit," Harrison muttered.

"She's probably a witch," Clinton called.

"I wish I had a bow and arrow right now," Kirk yelled, pointing his chainsaw blade at Clinton. "I'd put one right through your damned shoulder."

The silverback shifter was apparently done with Clinton's shenanigans after he'd attacked Harrison unprovoked last night. Or...not unprovoked, but for the stupid reason that Bash was getting that Meet-A-Mate party.

When Clinton lifted that dadgummed middle finger at Kirk, Bash stood, a feral snarl in his throat. Clinton ducked his head, his eyes warily on Bash as he tucked his fuckin' finger back again and returned to work.

Mason chuckled below them and muttered, "I can't wait to watch Bash kick your ass."

Bash forced the growl in his throat to taper to nothing and sat down again.

"Okay," Harrison said. "You said she wants to mother a stranger's get, but Bash, to a human, you two haven't known each other very long."

"I'm not a stranger," he muttered. He felt like he'd known Emerson for years. Like his life had been really little before she'd come into it.

Harrison sighed. "Look, for shifters things happen fast. We just know when we find the one. It don't work so easily for humans, and if she is already going in for an appointment, it means she's been wanting a baby for a long time and she's been going to doctors long before she met you. She probably didn't want to do the parenting thing alone, but she didn't meet the right partner."

"So you think I did wrong leaving last night?"

"No, I think your reaction was fair. That's a big blow. I know how bad you want cubs, and now the woman you want is trying to get pregnant by another." Harrison stripped a small branch off the log they sat on and broke it in half. "Bash, do you remember your real dad?"

"Yes," he gritted out, void of emotion.

"How was he to you and your mom?"

"He was an asshole. Didn't deserve her. Didn't deserve me. I clawed him up as soon as I was big enough and able."

"Yep. Now tell me about your stepdad."

"I love Bill." Bash crossed his arms over his chest and bit his bottom lip. "He came in when I was ten, and I was his, and my mom was his. I wish Bill was the real stock I came from."

"Is he still nice to your mom?"

Bash nodded hard once. "They've been together nineteen years, and he still buys her flowers every Monday and tells her nice things about the way she looks."

"And who sends you those funny birthday letters and cases of beer every October twenty-ninth?"

"Bill."

"And did he ever make you feel less important because you weren't his biological son?"

"No."

"Do you think you or your bear will be mad at Emerson's baby for being born with someone else's donated DNA?"

Oooh, he saw what Harrison was saying. He could be a Bill for Emerson's baby if he stayed friends with her. Bash scrubbed his hand down the stubble on his jaw as his thoughts raced around like a tornado. Okay, Emerson wasn't picking him back, but he didn't like the thought of her not being in his life. She wanted a smart daddy for her baby, and maybe that was okay. She laughed a lot at what Bash said, and not in a way that was making fun of him like kids used to do in school. She thought he was funny. It would be good if she had a smart baby. Bash imagined himself sitting in the front row when the kid played piano recitals and collected fancy awards, and no one would be prouder. He imagined Emerson's belly swollen with a baby, and the ache in his chest eased. Did it matter that the child would be another man's? It did, but how much? Would it be enough to keep him from being friends with Emerson? His life felt empty just thinking about it.

"I think I messed up," he said low. "Emerson was crying last night. Shit. She's probably scared to do this by herself, and I just left her there. I need the day off work tomorrow, Boss Bear."

Harrison gripped his shoulder and shook him slowly. "You got it."

SEVEN

Emerson choked down the horse pill the doctor had called pre-natal vitamins. She'd been taking them for months to prepare her body to grow a baby but, for some reason, this morning it was ridiculously hard to get down. She gagged and chugged water, then ate a cracker to bully the pill down her esophagus.

Maybe it was because she was nervous. She'd had chills since she woke up this morning and had peed about a billion times. She blew out a long, shaking breath as she looked at herself in the mirror. She was pale as a sheet, despite all the make-up she'd put on.

She was utterly alone.

Closing her eyes, she fought off another round of tears. Her family didn't support this decision, so they had refused to come to the appointment. But...hopefully she wouldn't be so alone after today. Emerson pressed her palms against her soft stomach and gave herself a tremulous smile in the mirror.

A knock sounded at the door, and Emerson frowned at the clock. *11:30*. She didn't have time to talk to solicitors, but she had ordered pregnancy tests in bulk online and was waiting on that delivery. Hopefully it was Mr. Mark, the friendly postal worker who still delivered door-to-door in this neighborhood.

With a plastered smile, Emerson opened her door and froze. The saturated midday sunlight was bright around Bash's wide shoulders. He stood straight-backed, much taller than her, but his weight was shifted to his back leg, as if he was uncertain of his decision to be here. In his hands was a small, floppy, black stuffed bear and a bouquet of bright pink roses wrapped in brown paper and twine.

"Don't tell me to leave," he said low.

"I won't."

"I'm sorry about the other night." His eyes were so incredibly bright, raw, and vulnerable right now. "I panicked, and I was hurt. I just wanted to get away from the pain, but not away from you." He handed her the bear and the flowers, and the corner of his lips turned

78

up in a hesitant smile. "Emerson roses, and that one is a bear, like me. My fur is black."

Emerson dragged a breath into her lungs, hugged the bear tightly to her chest, and clutched the wrapped flowers, blinking back the moisture that rimmed her eyes.

"It's for the baby, but you can snuggle it until he gets here. Or she." Bash shook his head like he was embarrassed. "The flowers are for you. Anyway, I want to take you to your doctor appointment if you'll let me. You should have a cheerleader waiting out in the sitting room when you're through."

To hide the single tear that was streaking down her cheek, Emerson stepped into the sunlight, slid her arm around his neck, and hugged him as tight as she could.

He hesitated for a moment, but then his hands rubbed up her back, and he rested his cheek against the top of her hair. In an instant, she felt good and whole and secure again. She'd thought she'd lost him. And yeah, it didn't make any sense for her to feel so attached to a man this soon, but some part of her had adored him since the day he'd paid her that genuine compliment in the library.

"I'd like for you to be in the waiting room," she whispered thickly. "I want that very much."

Taking his hand, she led him into her duplex. While she put her flowers in a vase, Bash looked at the pictures on her wall. "She looks like you," he said, pointing to Amanda.

"She's my younger sister. The kids are my nieces, and the guy with the big, goofy grin beside my sister in that top picture is my brother-in-law."

"Three cubs," he said, moving as he looked at each picture.

"Yeah, would you believe she was the one who never wanted a family? When we were growing up, my sister would give these elaborate speeches at the dinner table about how marriage was an outdated, meaningless ritual and that monogamy was unnatural and yada yada. But then she found Chris when she was twenty-one, and he changed her tune quick."

"But you always wanted kids," he murmured, squinting at a Christmas picture of her sister's family.

"Yeah, I wanted the family, but it didn't work out like it did for Amanda."

"Does that make you angry?"

"No. It makes me sad sometimes when I spend time with them because they're so happy. There is no loneliness in that family, you know? And I watch my parents with their granddaughters, and they're always asking when I'll settle down and give them more, like I haven't been trying for long-term relationships. And I don't know. Somewhere along the way, I just accepted it wasn't happening for me and decided to go get a family myself. My parents and my sister are frustrated with my decision to use a donor, but it'll be different when I have a baby. They won't remember how he or she came to be. They'll just love it."

"You're a strong woman," Bash said, honesty pooling in those striking eyes of his. "Strong and brave, and I like you even more now."

The stretch of her smile felt good after the last day of stressing about how they'd parted at the bar. She loved how he always said what he was thinking, and she loved even more that his head was full of nice thoughts. He was a good man. Maybe the best she'd ever met, and something inside told her she had only scratched the surface with him. "I don't want you to leave if I get pregnant," she admitted in a rush. Softer, she said again, "I don't want you to leave."

Bash was to her in an instant, and she gasped at how fast he was. His hand cupped her cheek. "I won't do that. I can't." Leaning into her, he kissed her lips, then pulled away with a sweet smack. His eyes were still closed when he eased back, but there was a smile on his lips now. "I forgot how good that feels with you." He inhaled deeply, and his shoulders relaxed on the exhale. "Come on now. I won't have you late to the doctor."

Feeling utterly drunk on that kiss, she set the vase of roses in the center of her kitchen table and floated after him in a daze. She almost forgot her purse, but remembered at the last minute when she didn't have her key to lock the door. Outside, Bash held out his elbow formally and pulled her hand against the crook.

"I like your dress," he said as he led her toward a gun-metal gray Dodge Ram.

Emerson looked down at her cream-colored sundress with the pink floral print. "It'll probably sound weird, but it felt right dressing up for this."

"Hell yeah. You're meeting the vial of your baby daddy's jizz today. One of those little tadpoles could turn out to be your baby. It's a big fuckin' deal."

She giggled and bumped her shoulder against his arm. God, she really liked Bash. A huge part of her still couldn't believe he was okay with this and supporting her, but under this big, burly, muscled-up exterior was a sweet and understanding man.

Bash winced against the sunlight and pulled a pair of aviator sunglasses off the V-neck of his black T-shirt. He put them on, then opened the door of his truck and helped her in. When she was settled, he closed the door and jogged around the front on his long, powerful legs. As he sat behind the wheel and turned on the engine, she realized something. Her baby wouldn't look anything like the man she loved. Loved? She stared at Bash's profile as he pulled out of her neighborhood. Strong jaw, straight nose, perfect dark scruff, and those gorgeous emerald eyes that lightened to such a mesmerizing color when his inner bear was close to the surface. He was perfect, but her baby would look different, like some blond-haired stranger. And now she was at about forty-two percent sure she wanted to go through with this.

There was a massive box in the back seat, and when she saw the picture on the side, she nearly choked on air. "Bash, did you buy a car seat?"

A soft growl rattled his throat. "Woman, you weren't supposed to guess what it is. I turned it so you couldn't tell."

"You didn't want me to know?"

"Well, my alpha said humans take things slower, and I don't want to rush you."

"What do you mean?"

"I pick you," he said with a shrug and a duh look.

"You pick me for what?"

Another growl, and he turned up the radio.

"Sebastian Kane, what the hell are you talking about?"

"You're my mate, and I'm only your friend, but I'm gonna hunt you until you give in, even if it takes a hundred years, and at some point in that hundred years, I'm gonna need a car seat in my truck for Bean."

"Bean?" she asked, utterly baffled.

"That's what I'm calling your baby until you name it."

"Oh," she said stunned as she stared back at the car seat.

"I researched it, and that's the safest one Saratoga has to offer."

Bash had just laid it on the line and admitted she was his choice. No one in her

BOARLANDER BASH BEAR | T. S. JOYCE

entire life had said anything like that. She'd fallen short with other relationships. They'd deserted her or picked other women, and she'd always been left feeling like not-quite-enough. But Bash was in this.

He not only had picked her, but he was choosing her future baby, too, by buying that car seat. Emerson hugged the stuffed bear against her middle to steady the nerves there.

Thirty-five percent. Shit, could she even do this anymore?

Yes. The last year of appointments and questions and planning had gotten her here to this day. This way Bash would have an out. They were new, and since it wouldn't be his baby biologically, he could still bow out. It was too early in their relationship to talk about building a family, and she was ready. More than ready. So why did she feel like puking all the sudden?

She gave Bash directions to the women's clinic and tried to anchor herself in the moment. It was normal to get cold feet. Dr. Mallory had said as much on multiple occasions, and that's all this was. Cold feet. And besides, there was a chance this wouldn't even take the first time. Wait. Was that what she wanted? For a baby not to take?

She felt like an ant in a toilet that someone had just flushed.

Bash rested his palm on her thigh and squeezed it gently. "You smell scared, but you don't have to be. I read on the Internet it won't hurt."

Sweet bear. She intertwined her fingers with his and lifted his knuckles to her lips. She kissed him there to reward him for being amazing.

At the women's clinic, she got out and straightened her dress, then clopped across the parking lot beside Bash. The air felt thin. And heavy. Unbreathable.

Bash led her through the sliding glass doors to the empty waiting room. "Slow day," she said with a nervous laugh.

"Hey Emerson," the nurse called from behind the check-in counter. "Dr. Mallory is ready for you if you want to come on back."

"So soon?" she squeaked out. "Okay." She offered Bash a smile, but it fell off her face with a lip tremble.

"It'll be okay. You'll make a good baby. Do you want me to hold that?" Bash asked, pointing to the stuffed bear she clutched to her stomach.

"Uhhh," she stalled, frowning down at the

soft present he'd gotten the baby. She hadn't realized she was still holding it. "I think I'll take it with me."

Bash gripped her shoulders and leveled her with a look. "I'll be right out here. We'll go get some fried pickles or whatever you want after this and have some fun, okay?"

"Yeah." Emerson hugged his waist and inhaled deeply. He smelled like a delicious combination of clean-breeze laundry detergent and masculine body wash. Gripping his shirt, she said, "I'll be right back," then eased away. She didn't look back as she signed in, or even when she followed the nurse out of the waiting room. She would fold if she did.

Dr. Mallory came in before she'd even had time to shut the door to room three. She carried a tray with an array of supplies and set them on the small counter by the sink. Emerson jerked her gaze away for reasons she didn't understand. Nothing on it had looked terrifying or painful, but she was having trouble coping with the fact that this was really happening. God, she'd waited so long for this day, and now she was freaking out? *Settle down, lunatic.*

"Okay," Dr. Mallory said brightly. "Put the gown on, and we'll have this done lickety-split."

"Lickety-split," Emerson repeated low. Just like that, and she would be done. The wait would begin. A couple of weeks, and she could take a pregnancy test and know if this worked or not. But she had this really strong feeling it would, and she now was at twenty-five percent.

"Oh, and Emerson?" Dr. Mallory asked before she left the room. "You're making the right decision with this sample. You'll have a really good chance at a viable, healthy baby. A baby, Emerson. Not an animal."

With a frown, Emerson asked, "What does that mean?" Her hackles were up but, damn it all, she didn't like the way Dr. Mallory had said that.

"I mean you will be able to have your baby anywhere and get him any kind of medical insurance and attention because he or she will be normal." Dr. Mallory shook her head like that should've been obvious.

"My child would be normal either way."

"No, Emerson." When the doctor's cheeks flushed red, her freckles disappeared into the color. "If your child was a shifter, it would be a freak. It wouldn't be natural." With an irritated sigh, she bustled out of the room and clicked the door closed behind her.

A freak? Stunned and angry, Emerson stared at the wall. Bash sat in that waiting room, just a few plaster barriers away, and he was sweet and caring, and a gentleman. He was no *freak*, and his children wouldn't be either. They would be lucky to have a daddy who cared so much about them.

Chest heaving, Emerson dragged her gaze to the stuffed bear in her arms. If she had a baby with a bear in him or her, would it be so bad? Bash had turned out just fine. In fact, every shifter she'd met at Sammy's seemed completely normal, happy, and content in each other's company. They hadn't made her feel *other* because she was human, even though they were probably made to feel that way all the time.

The long, syringe-like instrument on the tray taunted her. Was that what she needed to have a normal child? She didn't think so.

Zero percent.

Dr. Mallory knocked and came in. "You aren't dressed," she said, her ruddy brows furrowed.

"I can't do this," Emerson whispered.

"What?"

"I can't do this," she said louder, moving

89

toward the door.

"Emerson—"

"No, you listen to me. You have these judgmental, rude thoughts about shifters, but I love Bash. I *love* him, and he cares about what happens to me and a child I don't even have in my belly yet. He bought a damned car seat already. For a human, *normal* baby. So," she said, voice shaky and too high-pitched, "maybe you're the freak, and maybe you just aren't that nice, *Dr. Mallory*." She sidled the shocked looking woman and jogged down the hallway.

"But your sample!" Dr. Mallory called after her.

Emerson threw her an irritated wave over her shoulder. "Keep it."

She was angry and crying because everything was crumbling apart around her. Emerson stomped her flats against the tile floor and shoved the door to the waiting room open.

Bash was sitting in a chair, long legs outstretched, biting his thumbnail and looking utterly sick. He didn't want her doing this, but he'd come anyway. He stood in a rush and searched her face, worry slashing across his features.

Without a word, she ran over to him and

hugged his neck.

"It's okay," he said in a soft, confused tone as he rubbed circles over her back while she soaked his black T-shirt with her tears.

There would be no baby. Not now at least.

A sob wrenched from her throat, and Bash picked her up and carried her out of that clinic like she weighed nothing at all. He didn't say a word, just set her in the passenger's seat of his truck and watched as she wiped her cheeks with her fingertips.

"Did it hurt you?" he whispered in a broken voice.

"Promise not to be mad at me," she murmured.

"I promise. What is it?"

"I couldn't do it. I couldn't go through with it. I don't want a baby like this anymore."

Bash stood up straight, and his eyes went round. "What do you mean? You don't have a baby in your belly?"

"This is all I've wanted for so long, but then I met you, and you're nice and good to me and perfect. I don't want some stranger's baby. I want a family, and I'd convinced myself a baby was all I could have, but you make me want more. You make me want everything."

"But...I can't give you smart babies,

Emerson."

"Bash," she said, cupping his cheeks. "You're so smart. You're so good. You will make a wonderful father someday. I like *everything* about you."

Bash leaned into her palm and ducked his gaze. "I ain't smart like that donor. Not book smart."

"So? I'm not creative, and I suck at public speaking. Everyone has stuff they have to work harder at than other things, and that's okay. To me, you're great."

Bash backed out of her touch and paced the concrete the length of his truck, running his hands through his hair. "So you're waiting on a baby."

"Yes."

He scratched his head and looked at the box in the back seat of his truck, then went back to pacing. "So I can pick you still?"

"Yes."

"Emerson, I planned a baby party," he rushed out. "I was going to take you back up to my trailer park and we're grillin' steaks and going swimming in the falls, and I made a Happy Baby Making Day banner, but there ain't no baby."

She let off a happy laugh at how thoughtful

he was. "Not yet."

"Woman, what does that even mean? You're mixing up my head."

She huffed an emotional laugh and slid out of the truck, then hugged his waist to keep him from pacing again. "You want to date me?"

"Date you," he murmured. His heartbeat was pounding hard and fast against her cheek. "No, I want to mate you. Wife you. Fuck, I don't know what it's called. I pick you."

"Well, I'm picking you back."

Bash eased out of her hug, head hung low, shaking it back and forth, his eyes locked on hers and blazing bright moss green. "Don't tease me with that."

"I'm not. I pick *you*, Bash. You're mine and I'm yours, and someday when we're good and ready, maybe we'll have a cub of our own. One who has a good heart like you and my wild hair, who knows? All I know is I don't want to do this alone anymore, Bash. I want to try with you." She gave him a slow, happy smile as everything in her world felt good and right again. "I pick us."

EIGHT

"Are you sure your alpha will be okay with me staying the night?"

Bash stopped humming along with the radio and turned the wheel with one hand until they were off the main road and driving along a washed-out, gravel lane. "Harrison? He'll be fine with it. It's Clinton we gotta worry about."

"Well, if Clinton has a problem with it, I can go back to Saratoga tonight. I don't mind. I really don't want to make any of your crew uncomfortable."

Bash grinned and gave her a boyish shrug. "You're mine. They have to get used to you. Besides, I'll be there, and Clinton is no match for my bear right now, plus Audrey is a freaking tiger shifter and she gets real protective. She's been lonely and achin' for a girlfriend up here."

"Even though I'm human?"

Bash laughed and shook his head like she was silly. "That don't make no difference. Gia is mated to the Gray Backs' alpha, Creed, and she is one-hundred percent human. She's raising a brawny little cub and nobody treats her any different. Except I remember to be more gentle when I hug her so I don't squish her like a blueberry. But other than that, she's just one of us."

A smile cracked Emerson's face. She liked the sound of that—being a part of something. Oh sure, she had a good job and a happy life, but she had been lonely since she'd moved back to Saratoga. She'd thought she would spend a lot of time with Amanda and her family, but her sister was busy with her life, and Emerson hadn't fit back into this place like she'd hoped.

"I'm excited but also a little scared to meet your crew. I'm scared of animals bigger than Chihuahuas."

Bash snorted. "You'll have to get over that fear, and quick." He leaned forward and gave a two fingered wave at something in the woods.

Emerson followed his gaze and gasped. A massive silverback gorilla moved slowly through the trees, walking gracefully on powerful arms and legs. The animal watched them pass with aloof eyes that glowed a strange blue color. He nodded his chin once, then turned back into the woods.

"That's Kirk. I think he's going to be my second best friend."

"He's nice?" she asked in a barely audible whisper. Her danged throat had closed up tight. The animal walked slowly enough, but he held a quiet power that convinced her he could beat his way straight through this truck with little effort.

"He used to not be. His people are fucked up, but he turned it around. Went up against the gorilla shifters knowing he was going to get killed for doing the right thing, but he did it anyway. Now he's real good. A good man, a good shifter. Quiet, though, so don't get your feelings hurt if he don't talk your ear off. I hope our cub has your eyes. I mean..." Bash frowned. "Audrey said I should take it slow and keep things to myself. Remind me to tell you what I think when you're ready for a cub, okay?"

Kirk forgotten, Emerson dragged her gaze to Bash and giggled. "It doesn't bother me when you say your thoughts. Why do you want our future cub to have my eyes?"

"Because they're all wild and gold and pretty, like sunlight comin' through the tree branches and speckling the ground. You even have brown spots in there, like cheetah eyes. Part of me hopes no one else has noticed so those specks can just be mine. My secret part of you no one else looks close enough to notice."

Stunned into silence, she opened her mouth but found no words so squeezed his hand, stalling to compose herself after such sweet sentiments. Bash was, in fact, the only one who'd ever said anything about her oddly-colored "cheetah eyes." She had a melting pot of different ethnicities in her heritage, and they had all come together to give her a unique coloring. "I would be happy if our cubs had your eyes," she admitted in a murmur. "The green in them is hard to look away from sometimes. They are my favorite color." Emerson lifted his big, calloused hand and nuzzled her cheek against his knuckles before she settled it back in her lap.

She was suddenly not scared to meet his crew anymore. Bash would keep her safe, and the prospect of meeting his friends was suddenly and truly thrilling.

"My favorite color is orange, and tonight I'm going to show you why," Bash promised as they pulled under a wooden sign. *Boarland Mobile Park* had been carved into it, but that had been crossed out with red paint and now read *Missionary Impossible*.

"I have to paint over that," he muttered. "Clinton and me used to fight somethin' fierce over whether girls should be allowed in the trailer park or not, and after one battle, I got pissed off and climbed up there and painted that. Harrison told me I should be ashamed, but I wasn't."

Emerson pursed her lips against the urge to laugh because Bash was frowning so seriously right now, but she got it. Missionary position impossible. Clever bear.

The trailer park was a disaster. There were six trailers lined up lengthways, three on either side of a pothole-riddled gravel road, and on the end, facing the entrance sign, was a bigger singlewide with cream paint and dark shutters. It had an appealing red door and a new, sprawling deck out front. "I love red doors," she said.

"That's ten-ten, and Beaston says it's full of magic."

Chills blasted up Emerson's arms. "Magic

how?"

"I don't know exactly, but if Beaston says something's true, it is. Audrey moved her stuff out of it and into Harrison's trailer yesterday," Bash said, pointing to the first mobile home on the right. "I want you to stay the night with me, but Audrey said, 'Slow down, Bash Bear,' and she's smart, so I'll set you up in ten-ten for the night. Plus, if it has magic, I want that good mojo on you."

"Are you superstitious?" she asked through a grin.

"Not *super*stitious. Just a little-stitious."

God, she loved the way he thought and said things. He was so funny and sincere. And amazing. Definitely amazing.

All the trailers looked run down except for the one Bash slowed in front of. Middle on the left, it stuck out with its squares of new, bright green sod lined over the lawn, fresh mulch, and flowers and shrubbery on either side of a gorgeous deck with two rocking chairs. A pair of bright pink flamingos had been stuck into the yard, and a yellow sprinkler was gyrating slowly back and forth, watering the new grass. The trailer itself looked like the others. Singlewide, chipped white paint, crooked shutters, dilapidated roof, but at least it wasn't as destroyed as the one on the end on the right.

That one looked like a tornado had demolished half of it, and a blue tarp had been thrown haphazardly over a gaping hole where an entire wall was missing.

"What happened to that one?"

"Clinton," Bash said, but didn't offer any further explanation so she dragged her attention back to the pretty yard as Bash pulled between two trailers and parked his truck under a rusty metal carport.

Bash cut the engine and told her, "Wait there, so I can be a gentleman." He strode around the front of the truck and opened her door, and lands! Her heart was too big for her chest with how thoughtful he was being.

"So, since you don't have a baby in you, I don't have to be as gentle, right?"

"Uh, I guess?"

"Good, get on my back koala-style so your shoes don't get muddy, and I'll give you a tour of Bash Mansion."

Well, thank goodness she'd changed out of her dress and into cutoff shorts when he'd taken her by the duplex to pack an overnight bag. "This pretty one is yours?" she asked, scrambling onto his back.

"Sure is." Bash held the back of her knee at his hip with one hand and shut the door with the other. He grabbed her pink duffle bag out of the bed of his truck and strode toward the front of his trailer. "This place is a shithole, but Harrison finally made the call to clean this place up so it will attract mates. I ordered a bunch of supplies from down in Saratoga, but they haven't been delivered yet. I wanted to make sure my place was pretty for you, though. Look," he said, nodding with his chin toward the bright pink knock-out roses beside the porch. "Emerson roses."

"You named them for me?"

"Of course. They ain't as pretty, but close."

She held on around his shoulders tighter, buried her face between his shoulder blades, and smiled against his T-shirt. "Wait," she said, realizing something. "Is that where you got the flowers you gave me?"

"My stepdad gives my mom flowers every Monday. She stays with him because he makes her happy. I'm gonna give you flowers, but on Fridays, because that's when I thought you were gonna get a baby put in you." He climbed the porch stairs with her and settled her on her feet at the top, then pointed to the pair of rocking chairs. "Some of the women in the

Ashe Crew make home decorations and sell
them at the flea market and online. They're
real good, real high quality at their work, so I
bought these yesterday."

On closer inspection, the rocking chairs
were painted an antique gray color and had
tough, white canvas fabric on the seats and
backs with little cartoon owls and bears. They
were both beautiful pieces, and Bash had put a
hardy outdoor rug down in a matching gray
color.

"I don't know shit about decorating, but
Riley came over from Asheland Mobile Park
and helped me. She's good at decorating stuff.
She said this porch would make a mate
happy."

There were flower pots hanging from
hooks on the rails of the porch, and as
Emerson ran her fingertips across the arm of
one of the gorgeous rocking chairs, she smiled
up at Bash. "I like it very much."

Bash's lips ticked up, then fell. "I know I
don't have a lot to offer a lady like you. I know
this place looks like a dump," he murmured,
jerking his head toward the rest of the park.
"But we're right in the beginning of big
changes. Harrison is gonna be the alpha I
always knew he could be. If you give me time,

I'll make this a good place for you. And for cubs. Swing sets, stroller paths, a playroom, sandboxes, the works. I have big plans. It'll just take some time. If I would've met you a few months from now, this place wouldn't be so embarrassing."

"You shouldn't be embarrassed," Emerson said, gripping his hands and allowing him to see the honesty in her eyes.

"But your house is fancy and clean."

"Yeah, but Bash"—she turned and gestured to the pine tree mountains that surrounded them—"my duplex has nothing on this view."

He canted his head and brushed a knuckle down her cheek, soft as a butterfly kiss. "I like the way you say things. You don't lie. You don't say things you don't mean. I can tell." His finger trailed fire down her neck, and then he traced her collarbone exposed under the thin straps of her purple tank top.

She blew a shaky breath and closed her eyes. His touch felt so overwhelmingly good. Bash pressed his lips against her neck, and she bowed against him. "I won't bite you," he whispered, a moment before he grazed his teeth gently across her sensitive skin.

Oh how her body was reacting to his kiss.

Knees knocking, heart pounding, hands tingling, every nerve in her body firing, and her panties were already soaking wet from the drive from Saratoga when he'd rested his hand on her thigh, rubbing slow circles against her skin.

"Oh, Bash," she whispered as he sucked on her neck and guided her backward, his hand on her waist.

A soft rumble emanated from him, but she wasn't scared. His inner animal sounded content, not angry. "I like when you say my name like that, all quiet and needy," he murmured against her neck as he pushed the unpainted door of his trailer open.

Inside, Bash closed the door and pressed his lips to hers, pushed his tongue against hers. Emerson went completely pliable in his capable hands. She slipped her fingertips under the hem of his shirt and touched the warm skin right above his hip bones.

Bash jerked his pelvis and chuckled into her mouth. With a sexy smack of his lips, he eased away and said, "That tickled. If you're going to touch me, woman, mean it." Eyes locked on hers, he pulled his shirt slowly over his head, his eight-pack rippling and flexing with his movement. Emerson gave a slow, stunned blink at his Adonis body, but a puckered, uneven mark on his shoulder drew her attention. She reached for it, hesitated inches away, then pressed the pad of her fingertip to the scar. Bash searched her face with a troubled look but didn't flinch away.

"What's this?" she asked.

His Adam's apple dipped low in his throat as he swallowed hard. Softly, Bash answered, "Dragon's fire."

Sadness pooled in his eyes now and something more. Disappointment, perhaps. Slowly, she turned him and gasped when she saw his back. Bash had been badly burned.

"I don't like people seeing it. Especially not Harrison."

"Why not?" she asked, pressing her palms against his hot skin.

"Because I got it trying to save him."

"Trying to save him," she whispered. Harrison was still alive, so Bash had succeeded.

"I got it saving him," he corrected himself. "I don't want him to feel bad, so I keep it hidden. And I don't like the way it looks."

Emerson's eyes burned, and she blinked hard. She couldn't even imagine the pain he'd been in to heal from burns like these. She wrapped her arms around his waist and rested her cheek against his scarred skin. "I like the way it looks, but I understand. I don't like things about my body either. You don't have to worry about what I think, though, Bash. You are perfect. You are the most beautiful man I've ever seen, and I'm the luckiest that you picked me."

His back relaxed under her cheek, and he slid his giant hand over hers where she hugged his stomach. "What don't you like about your body?"

Her cheeks heated, but he had been brave by showing his secret self, so she would find courage for him. "I'm soft. See?" She pulled off her tank top and cut-off shorts and then squeezed her eyes closed so she wouldn't be embarrassed by his reaction. She'd only fooled around with boyfriends with the lights off, and Bash's living room was streaked with sunlight filtering through the half-open blinds of the back window.

He didn't say a word, but his hand brushed down her ribs. She flinched as he ran his touch across her belly, and when he reached around her and unsnapped her leopard print bra, she squeaked in mortification.

"Open your eyes," he whispered.

BOARLANDER BASH BEAR | T. S. JOYCE

She huffed a scared breath and braved a look at him. His head was canted, and his eyes reflected oddly, like an animal's in firelight. The color there was lighter and brighter, but that didn't mask the awe reflected in them. He pulled her palm and pressed it onto his erection, tight against the seam of his jeans. It was huge and hard as a rock. "You don't have to be scared in front of me. I've never seen anyone more beautiful."

"You don't mind if I'm...soft?"

Bash grinned as he dragged her waist against his. "Woman, you're shaped like a number eight. That's my favorite number." He cupped her breast and shifted their weight slowly to one side. "I like your soft parts the most."

"But...you look like a fitness model, and I'm...I don't know. I'm not magazine-model beautiful."

Bash pulled her closer and hugged her tight against his chest, swaying in a sweet, slow dance that was putting her insecurities to rest step-by-step. "You're beautiful when your face lights up in that easy smile. And when you laugh *with* me, not *at* me. You're beautiful in that tank top and cutoffs, owning your sexy body. You're beautiful when you're nice to people. Beautiful wild hair and perfect curves, and those cheetah eyes that light up when you see me. No, you don't look like a magazine model. You look better."

Her heart was now a puddle on the floor. It had vacated her body and melted, and now she was really going to cry. How had she lived her entire life without Bash? Her bone-deep loneliness seemed so far away now with him holding her so tightly. She'd never felt so happy or safe in her entire life.

Pushing upward on her tiptoes, she kissed him and wrapped her arms around the back of his neck, then whispered, "I like you."

Bash chuckled and lifted her off the ground. "I know."

"Cocky," she accused through a grin.

"Not cocky—you smell like sex and happiness. I did that. You like me."

She cracked up and nodded. Touché. Bash with his heightened senses and brutal honesty would never make it easy for her to play coy. Huh. She really liked the idea of no games with him.

Bash's blazing green eyes danced in the moment before he kissed her again, and when he settled her on her feet onto the cold laminate floor, he shocked her and slid his hand down the front of her panties. "Want to touch you," he murmured between kisses. He dragged two fingers up her wet folds, and she jerked against his hand accidentally. Before she could muster her embarrassment, he cupped her sex and slid a finger inside her. With a moan, she rolled her hips forward to bump her clit more firmly against his palm. The growl was back in his throat, more urgent this time. Hooking his free arm around her back, Bash carried her through the small kitchen and into his bedroom. She was lost in his kiss now, numb to the world as he worked her closer to orgasm. He pushed his tongue deep into her mouth just as he settled her on top of his soft bed.

"I'll take care of you," he whispered, easing back to shuck his jeans. "I know you don't want no baby with me now, and I don't have protection, so I'll just make you feel good, okay?"

"Okay, okay," she panted out as he pulled her panties down her thighs.

But she wanted more. Needed more. Bash had unsheathed his giant, throbbing dick, and it jutted out between his powerful legs as he positioned himself above her, straddling her hips. He would feel so good buried deep inside her, but maybe he was right. Maybe they should hold off trying for babies. She thought about her appointment, but all her reasoning from this morning flapped out the window like a colony of bats. They both wanted to be parents, and they both cared deeply for each other, but they were supposed to wait for...something.

Emerson spread her knees wider to give him more room in the cradle between her thighs. Needy, little beggar, she knew she was teasing and tempting, but she was losing her mind. The triceps of his muscular arm flexed as he locked his arm against the mattress, his hand right beside her face. He rocked his hips above her, as if he couldn't help himself, and slid two fingers into her.

She cried out at how good it felt and arched her back against the comforter, spreading her legs even wider.

"Fuck, Emerson," Bash whispered, eyes on her breasts. He leaned down and drew her aching nipple into his mouth, soothing it instantly as he lapped and sucked her, moving his fingers inside of her in a steady, slow rhythm.

Emerson leaned forward and gripped his hard shaft, then slid her hand down it. Bash tensed his abs and rocked forward, encouraging her touch, as he rolled his eyes closed. The head of his cock was swollen and red and a drop of moisture appeared on the tip. His hips bucked again as she took another stroke. God, he felt so good moving his fingers inside her, but her foggy mind screamed that it wasn't enough. Testing, she pulled his dick downward until it touched her sex.

Bash gritted his teeth then kissed her deeply, his tongue pushing against hers at the same pace he was setting with his fingers. Emerson kept his dick against her wetness until he lowered down farther and rubbed each stroke against her sex without her guiding him. Slowly, he withdrew his fingers and gripped her hips, shaft resting on top of her. So close, and not nearly close enough. She kissed his neck, then bit him gently before returning to his lips, and now Bash's control was slipping as he rolled his hips against her. He jerked back, and the head of his shaft touched her entrance, dipped in slightly.

Bash clenched his jaw and flinched his hips away. "I want to be in you so bad, but we can't. What if…"

Emerson cupped his cheek and searched his eyes. "What if something great happened?"

Bash frowned slightly. "Yeah."

"You want to try with me?" she whispered.

Bash's hips moved, and he slid shallowly into her again, which caused her to rock toward him. God, he would feel so good.

"You're sure?" he asked.

She leaned up and kissed him gently, then relaxed and nodded.

Bash let off a relieved sigh and dipped into her again.

"Deeper," she begged.

And he did. Bash wrapped his arm around her back and slid into her slowly, halfway, then back. She was so wet and ready. A soft, sexy growl vibrated from his chest as he pushed into her again, burying himself inside her. Easing out, he kissed her. She nipped his bottom lip and held him between her teeth as he flexed his abs against her and slid into her again.

"Oooh," she moaned, tossing her head back.

His lips were everywhere. Little bursts of fire enflamed her skin where he touched her, and now he was bucking into her faster, harder. She was pushed farther up the bed with his force and was blinded by the intense ecstasy between her thighs. He was so big, so powerful, so perfect inside of her, as though he'd been made to be her perfect match, her perfect fit.

Bash buried his face against her neck and held her close as he slammed into her. She was so close.

"I'm coming, I'm coming," she whispered mindlessly.

Orgasm blasted through her in throbbing bursts just as Bash rammed into her and froze.

He cried out a sexy, helpless groan as his dick throbbed inside her, filling her with waves of heat with every pulsing shot of his seed. He moved again, slower, smoother as her clenching body matched his release. Nothing had ever felt so good, so right.

Bash stroked into her slowly for a long time until every last aftershock was done, and then he smiled against her neck. He eased out and slid down her body until his chin was on her stomach. With an adoring smile, he murmured, "I know I'm supposed to go slow, but I like you, too. I mean...I *like* you." His eyes were raw and conveyed something much deeper, pleaded for understanding, and she got it.

With a happy smile, she pulled a pillow under her head so she could see him better.

Running her fingernails through his dark, mussed hair, she admitted, "I love you, too, Bash Bear."

His lips twitched into a smile, and then he sighed a long, relieved sound. He kissed her belly gently, then murmured, "You said you're the luckiest, but you're wrong. You give me everything. You make me the lucky one."

NINE

Bash's heart was beating fast against her cheek as he lay under the covers with her. Emerson had been lost in happy thoughts, watching a square of light from the window travel slowly up the foot of the bed toward them, but Bash's pulse should've slowed by now. They'd been quiet for a while, just cuddling.

He pulled her in closer against his side, and it happened again. His heart rate galloped. Narrowing her eyes, she rested her chin on his chest and asked, "Sebastian Kane, what on earth are you thinking about?"

His eyes flew wide, but he only met her gaze for a moment before he looked away. "I'm happy, and then I feel bad, and then I'm happy again."

Tracing the burn mark on his shoulder,

she whispered, "Tell me why you're happy first."

"Because you want a cub with me."

She smiled and said, "Now tell me why you feel bad."

"Because my dad was dumb, and I'm dumb, too. You're smart, and you wanted a smart dad for your cub. You settled. And then I think you don't mind because you never made me feel simple, but then I don't want you to be mad later if our cub ain't smart. I didn't make good grades in school. I mean, in math I did because I understand numbers, but English and language arts and history and all the others... My mom just about pulled her hair out trying to help me pass."

"I bet you were good at gym."

"I was fuckin' awesome at gym," he said, eyes serious. "And lunch. I beat all the kids at lunch."

She stifled a laugh and clamped her teeth on his chest, then said, "Now ask me how I feel."

Bash brushed her corkscrew curls away from her face and then tried but failed to tame them behind her ear. "How do you feel?"

"I feel happy, then bad, then happy again," she said, using his answer.

"Why happy?"

"Because it feels like my whole life—all the hard stuff, and the easy stuff, and the crooked road to my twenty-eighth year—led me right here into your arms. And then I think about us trying for a baby and it makes me excited and warm inside. In my chest, where my heart is."

"I feel that, too. Warm and good." His brows lowered. "Why bad?"

"Because you don't see yourself the way I see you. You aren't dumb, Bash. You're fun, hilarious, and kind, and so much smarter than you give yourself credit for. I feel bad because I don't like you talking about yourself that way. And then I feel happy again when I think about our cub being like you someday."

The frown lifted from his features and was replaced by one of those crooked, heart-stuttering smiles. "What do you mean, someday?"

With a laugh, she said, "Well, it might not happen right away for us. We might have to try for a little while. Practice."

"I'm fine with practicing," he said immediately. His attention shot to the square of light, now resting on their hips. "The others will be off their shift soon. Do you want to see ten-ten?"

She gave him a suspicious glare. "Are you trying to rub its magic off on me?"

Nonchalantly, he said, "Maybe," then kissed her forehead and rolled out of bed. "Also, I really did set up a party for you down by Bear Trap Falls, and I need to get cooking or everyone will be bitchin' about me taking too long. We come off that mountain hungry."

"Hmmm," she said happily as she slid from the bed and rooted around for her panties. When she saw the tattered fabric, she gasped and held up the pitiful negligee. "Bash, you ripped them!"

"Well, I was gentle with everything else." He snatched them out of her hand. "Besides, these are mine now. Audrey taught me how to scrapbook."

"What? No! You aren't putting my panties into a scrapbook!"

He laughed and held them too high for her to reach. "These are for the When Bean Was Made page."

Mortification blasted heat through her cheeks as she jumped, trying to reach them.

Bash flicked them up in the air out of her reach. "For real, Emerson, I want them. I won't scrapbook them if you don't want me to."

She stopped bouncing and rested her

palms against her cheeks to cool the burn. "Then why do you want them?"

He cocked his head and frowned like she should know the answer already. "To smell later, obviously."

"Oh, my gosh, I can't even have this conversation," she said, making her way into the living room where her duffle bag sat near the front door.

"It's like pheromones with a hint of soap," he murmured.

"Stop smelling them, Bash!"

"I'll give you a trade." Bash appeared in the living room empty-handed. He'd probably already hid the damned panties in his room somewhere.

"I don't want your underwear."

"How about a sleep shirt?"

She narrowed her eyes and tried to cling to that wisp of anger, but it faltered like a mirage in a desert when he grinned at her. His happiness was infectious. Bash pulled his black cotton T-shirt off the floor and handed it to her.

After a moment of hesitation, she begrudgingly took it and sniffed his shirt. It smelled of cologne and body wash that was probably named Sexy Lumberjack or Cool

Evergreen or Biker Bear Mutton Chops or some other manly name. It smelled divine. "Fine. Trade accepted."

"Great. Now come on. I have to get you settled into ten-ten. It takes a long time to heat pizza rolls on the grill."

She huffed a surprised laugh as he disappeared back into his bedroom. One thing was for sure and for certain. Life with Bash would never be dull.

After she was decent again with her bathing suit under her clothes and hair pulled in a mess of curls on top of her head to cover up the mega-sex-hair she'd been rocking, she glossed her lips, reapplied mascara, and spun to leave his bathroom. On second thought, she turned to a full-length mirror and lifted her tank top, then pressed her hands on her belly. Today had gone so differently than she'd imagined, and the promise of a new life and adventure filled her stomach with butterflies. Even if it took them a while to get pregnant, just the thought of starting this journey with the man she loved was exciting. Mom and Dad would flip out, and Amanda, too, of course, because Emerson wasn't doing things the conventional way, but so what? She was really and truly happy, and that would have to be good enough for her family.

"Em. Emmy. Emalemadingdong," Bash muttered from the other room.

With a laugh, Emerson tugged her shirt back into place and sauntered into the other room where Bash was tying the front of his low-slung, green and white swim trunks.

"What are you saying?" she asked, utterly amused.

"I'm seeing if I like any nicknames for you."

"Well, I vote no on Emalemadingdong."

"I like your real name best," he agreed, slipping into a pair of flip-flops and pulling on a white T-shirt. "Hey, we match!" Bash pointed to the strap of her green bikini top that showed under her tank. "Clinton is gonna be so mad 'cause we're so fuckin' cute. We should take selfies and tape 'em to his trailer. I like your lip glitter."

Yep, from this day forth, Emerson was definitely going to call lip gloss "lip glitter."

Bash swooped in and kissed her laughter away, then eased back with a big grin on his face. He squeezed her shoulders and gave a silent, excited shake of his head, then released her and pulled her by the hand toward the living room. "I'm gonna tell everybody what we did in my bed."

"Nope."

"Fine, I'm going to tell everyone we made out, but wink a lot so they get what I really mean."

"Bash, no."

"Fine, I'll draw a picture of us doing it."

"No."

"Sign language."

Giving up, she sighed through her smile as he picked up her bag and opened the front door.

"No answer means yes. I made this!" he said, pointing to the door. "It used to be just a stack of tires on account of Poop Chute Clinton saying I couldn't fix up the trailer, but now I have a door. I made it fancy for you," he murmured, standing back to look at his handiwork. "I'll paint it red because you said you like red doors. No animals will get in." His lips pursed into a thin line. "I will miss kicking the tires down, though."

Bash jogged down the stairs and held his arms out, waiting for her to koala bear him again. As she climbed on his back, he said, "I'm going to make you a walking path. You have to almost drown sod for it to take here, so it'll be wet and squishy for a while, and your shoes will get messed up."

She nibbled his earlobe. "They're just flip flops."

Bash straightened out her leg. "But your toenails are painted all pretty."

She wiggled her toes so the glossy fire-engine-red polish shone in the sunlight. "You like them?"

"Hell yeah. They make me imagine us watching TV on my couch late at night with your feet resting in my lap, and then we fuck."

She cracked up and hugged his neck tighter as he walked easily across the yard, ducking the sprinkler water. "Are all of your imaginings going to end with us fooling around?"

"Yes. I almost forgot to tell you. There is a mouse in ten-ten." Bash settled her on her feet on the white gravel road. "You aren't afraid of them, are you? I mean you said you were scared of animals bigger than Chihuahuas, and Nards is definitely smaller, so you're good, right?"

A mouse? "I'm a little scared of them." Try, a *lot* scared of them.

"Audrey says he's real polite, and he never gets up on the counters or the furniture so long as she puts food somewhere on the floor for him. He likes grapes best. The green kind, not the purple. He's tame as a pet store mouse."

"And his name is Nards?" That sounded less scary than Rabid Monster Field Mouse, which is what she would've named it.

Bash pulled the strap of her duffle bag across his chest and draped an arm around her shoulders. "I promise you'll be okay. All the girls in the Ashe Crew and Gray Back Crew have lived in ten-ten, and no one had a single horror story about Nards. He's a lucky mouse."

"Maybe if I see him and it's not a surprise encounter, I'll feel better," she said doubtfully.

Bash kissed the side of her head and sounded proud when he declared, "Brave mate."

"Mate?" The butterflies in her stomach had turned to falcons.

"Yes. But slow, I forgot. Girl...friend. That doesn't sound like enough."

"No, no, you can call me 'mate.' Is that the terminology for shifters when you pair up?"

"Yes. I was always scared my bear wouldn't pick. I mean, I knew he was ready because I've been fighting these instincts to go meet women, but it's the animal's choice first."

"And your bear picked me?"

"We both did. You are the easiest choice I

ever made. Harrison said it would be like that, but you just don't know for sure until it happens to you. I felt sick at the Meet-A-Mate Bash. All I wanted to do was be with you, and when we had our fight, I just wanted to go home. I watched you leave, and you were crying. It felt like my guts were getting cut out of my body and then set on fire and then peed on and then put back in my body. And then it felt like someone ran over me with a tractor."

"I'm really glad that didn't actually happen to you," Emerson said, feeling a little queasy at the mental image.

"My chest used to be all tight," he said, turning to walk backward in front of her. "Now it don't hurt at all."

"Because of me?" she asked, touched at how honest and sweet he always was to her.

"Yeah." He inhaled deeply. "You make me breathe easy."

"Will I ever get to see your bear?" she asked. "Or is that against the shifter laws?"

"Do you want to see him?" Bash asked, his face going solemn as he stepped into line beside her again.

"Yeah."

"You'll be scared. He's...different than me."

"Is he mean?"

"No, just dominant, and he don't mind fighting. You'll make him more protective."

"Will he hurt me?"

"Never. You're mine to protect. I'll always keep you safe, no matter what."

And she believed him. Bash was optimistic, fun-loving, and open, but he was also as tall as a redwood and built like a Mack truck. If he thought his bear was beastly, then he was, simple as that. Bash didn't sugarcoat things. He just said it like it was and moved on.

What would she do if anyone tried to hurt Bash? Red-hot boiling anger flooded her veins at the thought. He was good, kind, and wouldn't hurt anyone unprovoked. That stupid article she'd edited for Bartleby flashed across her mind, and she got even angrier. Bartleby didn't know anything, and he was definitely going to be pissed when he saw what she'd done to his article. She was probably going to get fired as an editor, but suddenly, she didn't care so much about that. Spending time with Bash had shaped her dream job into something new. She didn't want to edit anti-shifter articles anymore. She wanted to *write* for the newspaper and show Saratoga the other side to shifters that Bartleby had failed to see.

The thought of submitting articles of her own had been on her mind for a while now, but this right here was the exact moment she decided to go to battle for the shifters of Damon's mountains. It was the moment she decided to protect Bash the only way she knew how—by publically opposing the anti-shifter murmurings that had sprouted up in Saratoga when humans had learned that dragon shifters existed.

Hugging Bash's arm and resting her cheek against him, she promised, "I'll keep you safe, too."

TEN

Gooseflesh rippled across Emerson's arms as she stepped through the front door of 1010. Maybe it was just because Bash had been so adamant about there being magic here. The old singlewide looked clean, from the sagging white ceiling to the white walls to the dark, cheap laminate wood floors. It was swept and smelled of kitchen cleaner. The furniture was sparse but went well. There was a green couch to match a green loveseat. A tiny eat-in area with a dark table and two chairs sat adjacent to the white cabinet kitchen with faux wood countertops. So what if there were stains on the ceiling where leaks had been patched, and the floors were a little rotted and squishy as she made her way through the kitchen to the bedroom? This place was downright homey.

"I can ask Willa to paint a picture of us,"

128

Bash said. "She's real good. Audrey had her picture with Harrison hung right there." He pointed to the long wall on the back of the trailer. "That way it'll break up all that white paint. Or I can ask Riley to make you something to hang on a nail there. She and those Ashe Crew girls are real creative. Shabby chic stuff, or so they call it. The ladies at the flea market go mad for it." Bash shrugged and dropped his gaze. "Or something."

"I like that you went to so much effort to make this place good for me."

"Well, someday I want you to stay. Here. With me. I know you have your own place in Saratoga, and your work is there, too, but I like the idea of getting to sleep next to you, wake up with you, and kiss your forehead before I go to work in the mornings."

He'd painted such a beautiful picture that she hugged his waist as a thank you. Every man she'd ever met had been aloof and had kept her at arm's length, but Bash had no qualms with saying exactly how he felt.

"Knock, knock." A brunette with glossed lips, a high ponytail, and dancing brown eyes came in the front door. She clasped her hands in front of her pink T-shirt that read *Moosey's Bait and Barbecue*, and then rushed forward

BOARLANDER BASH BEAR | T. S. JOYCE

and held out her hand for a shake. "I'm Audrey, proud mate to Harrison Lang, Second in the Boarlanders, tiger shifter, and I'm really, really glad you're here."

Emerson grinned and shook her hand. "I'm Emerson Elliot. Uuuh, human, really glad to be here and..." She looked shyly at Bash and shrugged her shoulders as she murmured, "Proud mate to Sebastian Kane."

"Oh my stars, are you serious?" Audrey's voice had pitched to a decibel that was just under a dog whistle and Bash covered his ears. "Bash!" She shook his shoulders. "You picked!"

Bash chuckled and pulled both Emerson and Audrey in for a bear hug. "I picked a while ago, but I had to wait for her to catch up."

"Wait, wait, wait," Audrey said, going soft beside Emerson. "Bash, we have to be careful. She just had her procedure today."

Oh yeah. Bash was throwing her a Happy Baby Making Day party, and he wasn't a subtle man, so probably all the Boarlanders knew about her doctor appointment this morning. Heat flashed up her neck and into her cheeks.

"Right," Bash said, loosening his death-grip and letting them out of the hug.

Emerson thought he would tell Audrey about them trying for a cub because he looked all bright-eyed and feverish with excitement, but he gave her a wink and zipped his lips instead. Relief slid over Emerson's shoulders. She wanted to clutch onto their little secret for a while longer to keep the pressure off in case she didn't get pregnant right away.

"I'm really excited to have another girl in the trailer park," Audrey said. "I love the boys, but it'll be nice having a conversation that doesn't involve sex or toots."

Emerson giggled and said, "Too bad for you that's all I talk about."

"Perfect," Audrey teased. "I have to show you something I found this morning when I moved the rest of my stuff out." She pulled Emerson by the hand through the large bedroom on the other side of the kitchen to a bathroom at the end of the trailer.

"I hope you didn't move out because of me," Emerson said, suddenly worried that she'd caused much more chaos here than she'd realized.

"No, you just gave me the push. I've been sleeping over at Harrison's for a while now. I was ready to make the move official." Audrey flashed her a friendly smile and squatted down in front of a pair of white-washed cabinets under the bathroom sink. She pulled the door open and gestured to something inside. "Look."

Emerson knelt beside her and peered inside, then froze. Against the back left corner was a nest of grass, shredded paper plates, and pillow stuffing, and inside it, there was a gray mouse with three little, hairless, pink, wriggling babies suckling on her. Emerson's fear of mice was currently warring with her awe at the new lives she was seeing.

"I assumed Nards was a boy," Emerson whispered so as not to disturb the little family.

"This isn't Nards," Audrey said, matching her quiet tone. "This is his lady-mouse, Nipples."

Bash knelt down behind them and leaned over Emerson's shoulder. "Nards had babies?"

"Yeah, look." Audrey pointed to the other side of the cupboard where a hole had been chewed in the side, and sure enough, a mouse with giant testicles was dragging a potato chip toward the nest.

"What a good daddy," Emerson crooned softly as she watched the sweet little family. Nipples and Nards were taking good care of their tiny wiggly peanuts.

Bash would be a good father like Nards someday.

As if he could read her mushy thoughts, Bash leaned in and kissed the side of her hair. "Now do you believe me?"

"About what?"

He locked his gaze on her and smiled. "About ten-ten being magic."

Wide-eyed and heart thumping against her chest, Emerson dragged her attention back to the little family. Any other day of her life, she would've been terrified of these field mice, but today was different. Maybe it was because the mice barely paid attention to the three of them, or maybe it was because Emerson was flanked by a freaking bear shifter and a tiger shifter, and a mouse was the least terrifying animal in the room.

Or maybe, just maybe, Bash was right because this place certainly *felt* important.

Emerson cradled her stomach and smiled emotionally.

Maybe 1010 really was magic.

ELEVEN

Audrey was one of the nicest people Emerson had ever met. She'd given her a tour of the trailer, told her all the tricks to get it working in top shape, and had filled the pantry and glossy, new-looking fridge with food. She'd even told her which snacks Nards liked best, which was why Emerson was placing a jalapeño-flavored potato chip on the kitchen floor right now.

She would've just given it directly to Nipples, but she had the distinct feeling that Nards liked to actively take care of his family. Respect.

Next time she was at the store in Saratoga, though, she was going to get some seeds and mouse food from the pet store to make sure Nipples and Nards had a balanced diet.

"You hear that?" Bash asked from the

kitchen table.

"No."

"Oh, I forgot you have dull human senses. The boys are off-shift and coming down from the mountains."

"I do not have dull senses. They are just not as heightened as yours." She stuck her tongue out and re-tied her loose bikini top behind her neck.

"Come here, pitiful human," he said through a baiting grin.

Bash pulled her up against his chest and hugged her gently. Too gently. He was barely touching her, which made her giggle. Bash wasn't naturally a careful man. He was a stomping, clumsy beefcake who sloshed drinks and broke stuff regularly, but with her, he moved in slow motion, like she was a butterfly protectively cupped in his hands.

That's how she could tell Bash loved her.

Emerson laid tiny, pecking kisses all across his chest until she could feel the vibration of his deep chuckle against her lips. She adored the sound of his happiness.

"Come on," he murmured, massaging the back of her neck gently. "I can't wait to show you off to my crew."

"I like Audrey," she said as she followed

him out of 1010.

"She likes you, too, I can tell. Audrey had it real lonely growing up. She didn't know any shifters, and she had to hide what she was. She's been sore for a girl in the park."

"That sounds terrible, having to hide all the time." She knew about heart-deep loneliness from the last couple of years in Saratoga, but having to endure it for most of a lifetime? That could turn a happy person dark, but Audrey was sweet as pie. Emerson respected her even more now.

Out on the porch, she grinned again at how pretty Bash's landscaping and yard were. She couldn't get over how he'd planted roses that reminded him of her and fixed this place up to prepare for a mate and family. Sure, this trailer park had a lot of work to go, but it was exciting to see it at the beginning stages of change. Someday, she had a feeling this place was going to be amazing, and she was going to have the privilege of seeing that transition.

And as she waved to Audrey who was coming out of the first trailer that she shared with Harrison wearing a big greeting grin and a giant tote bag, it struck Emerson that fate had lent a hand in her being here today.

Everything had fallen into place and just in

time for her to balk against the artificial
insemination that would've taken her life in a
completely different direction. Now she was
trying for a baby with a man she loved more
and more with every minute she spent with
him, and she was building a friendship with
Audrey. Not a pretend one like with Dana at
the diner, but an actual camaraderie where
she and Audrey could bond because they were
going through this adventure with the
Boarlanders together.

Bash, Audrey, the trailer park, 1010,
Nards, and Nipples, all of it—her life was
richer now than it had ever been. It had all
happened so quickly Emerson was dizzy with
the hard right turn her life had taken. All she
could do now was hang on tight and enjoy the
ride.

A tall man with chin-length chestnut hair
and dark eyes came out of the trailer next
door, pulling a shirt over a set of washboard
abs. Geez, everyone here had beast-mode
bodies. Emerson self-consciously pulled at the
hem of her tank top, but Audrey sauntered
their way in nothing but a pair of cut-off shorts
that looked a lot like Emerson's and a triangle
bikini top on display. Audrey had curves, too,
but she strutted up to them like her self-

esteem was doing just fine. Right on. Emerson stood straighter and stopped fidgeting with her shirt. It was really hard to have low self-esteem when Bash was pulling her back against his chest and poking her in the crack with his boner. Between him and Audrey, Emerson was going to come out of this trailer park about as big-headed as they came.

"What are you giggling at?" Bash asked.

"I just like it here is all."

"Good." He sounded pleased as punch. "Emerson, this is my second best friend, Kirk." He gestured to the man approaching them.

"You're the gorilla shifter," Emerson blurted out accidentally.

Kirk gave her an easy smile and shook her hand. "I am. Nice to meet you, Emerson. I've heard a lot about you."

"You have?"

"Oh yeah, your man won't shut up about you," Kirk said with a wink at Bash.

"Wait, I thought you were on shift today," Bash said, a frown in his voice.

Kirk cast a glance at the back of the trailer park to a little road that sliced between 1010 and another trailer. "Harrison sent me home."

"Why the fuck did he do that? We haven't been hitting our numbers. He was already short with me going to Saratoga today."

"Clinton and I got into it." Kirk turned and lifted his shirt up to show four healing red slashes across his back. "Harrison wanted to send Clinton's dumb ass home, but I was so pissed I couldn't Change back. And as you can imagine, my gorilla wouldn't be safe with a chainsaw, so Harrison waved me off."

Bash snorted. "You should get Willa to paint you a picture of your gorilla holding a chainsaw under a rainbow. That shit would be funny."

Emerson pursed her lips against a smile because Kirk had been hurt by one of his own crew, and not all was puppies and glitter in the Boarland Mobile Park. The fact that the boys were joking about this so easily meant fighting wasn't a rare occurrence. And she was human, in a crew of beasts.

"Don't worry," Audrey said, settling in beside her. "We won't let anything happen to you, so you can stop your scared smell. Bash is a brawler, and so is Kirk."

"And Audrey will straight-up maim his ass if he gets out of line," Bash muttered. "She didn't get Second by a vote. She earned it with her claws."

Emerson tossed Audrey a shocked look.

Okay, knowing that Audrey was a tiger shifter and actually thinking about this woman carving out a place with these rough-and-tumble Boarlanders was unsettling. She was so nice, but maybe her beast wasn't as sweet, and that was intimidating as hell.

"Your face looks so freaked out right now," Audrey said through an amused smile. "Hey, look, I wore green to match."

She popped the string of her white and green polka dot bikini, and just like that, Emerson relaxed. Audrey might be a shifter, but she'd never given her a reason to be scared.

A bright red, jacked-up pickup truck with black rims and fat tires bumped and bounced past the trees and through the back entrance of Boarland Mobile Park.

"There's my man," Audrey said, waving.

Harrison gave her a two-fingered wave from where his hand rested on the steering wheel. He pulled on through and came to a stop in front of them, parking right in the grass, just barely missing the new sod of Bash's yard.

A dirty blond giant of a man with sparking gray eyes jumped out of the back of the truck, and a dark-haired man with blazing blue eyes slid out from the passenger's seat. He looked tired and irritated, his face streaked with sweat and dirt. The T-shirt under his flannel was soaked straight through, but when he saw Emerson, he forced a smile. "You must be Emerson." His voice was hoarse like he'd been yelling all day, but he offered his hand for a shake, and his eyes slightly darkened from their inhuman, icy color. "I'm Mason."

"It's really good to meet you, Mason."

The blond wasn't so polite, though. He spat on the gravel road and hooked his hands on his hips. "Clinton," he gritted out under Harrison's glare.

"I'm Emerson." She held out her hand, but he only stared at it.

"You shouldn't be here—"

"Again?" Audrey snapped. "Seriously? Clinton, you can't stop anyone from pairing up. Stop being so fucking rude."

"None of you understand what's really happening," Clinton barked out. "Every time someone in these mountains pairs up and adds to our numbers, you put a fucking target on our backs."

Harrison sighed a pissed-off sound. "What are you talking about, man?"

Clinton shook his head for a long time, the

silence growing thick in the trailer park. "Did you go to the doctor today? Are you growing a human fetus or what?"

"Clinton!" Harrison barked out.

"It's fine," Emerson rushed, not wanting to be the cause of any friction in the crew. "No, I didn't go through with it. I need more time." And hell no, she wasn't ready to tell this rude man about trying for a cub with Bash. He would suck all the joy from their decision.

"Well, good," Clinton said low. "Bash can't be gentle enough for a baby, and you don't need anything tying his bear to you. He wouldn't leave you if you got pregnant, and now you can still get away from him, too. Look, I can't stop you. I can't stop anything. I tried." He pulled her hand from her side and shook it startlingly hard. "Welcome to hell, Emerson, 'cause that's what this place will be soon enough." With one last fiery look for Bash, Clinton turned and strode for his trailer. The blue tarp flapped loudly as he slammed the door behind him.

"That actually went better than I thought it would," Harrison muttered, his dark blue eyes zeroed in on where Clinton had disappeared.

"Me, too," Audrey and Kirk said in unison.

Mason shook his head and said, "I need a

vat of beer to wipe today from my mind. Kirk,"
he said, swinging his attention to the goliath
beside Emerson, "you made the right decision
leaving when you did."

"Why is he being so ridiculous today?"
Audrey asked.

"The party for Emerson," Harrison said.
"He doesn't react well to change."

"This is my fault?" Emerson asked.

"No, it's his fault," Mason said, kicking at
an ant pile with the toe of his work boot and
crossing his arms over his chest. "Clinton likes
to fight everything."

"Should I go talk to him?"

"No," Bash and Audrey said in unison.

"Just let him be. He can come to the party
or not, his choice," Bash said in a strange,
monotone voice. "Come on. I need to fire up
the grill and feed you."

"I'll meet you out there," Mason said as he
strode for the middle trailer across the road.
"I'm gonna clean up first."

"I'll get you a vat of beer," Bash called
darkly.

He strode for his trailer, but Emerson
jogged and caught his hand. "Bash, Clinton is
wrong. You'll be plenty gentle with a baby."

When he turned around, Bash's eyes were

the dark color of pine needles, and he looked sick, as though he'd been socked in the stomach. "How do you know?"

"Because of how gentle you are with me." She shook her head and searched his sad eyes, then whispered, "He's wrong about everything, Bash. I'm not going anywhere."

TWELVE

Bash blocked out the entire sun with his wide back as he carried a giant blue cooler over one shoulder like it weighed nothing at all. Moments like these shocked Emerson. Bash was sweet and gentle with her, but she couldn't deny the raw power he wielded.

He hid his strength well in Saratoga, but up here in the wilderness, he let his animal side slip out more and more. She loved it.

He pushed a giant limb out of the way and waited for her to pass through before he let it go behind him. "I like this view better," he rumbled, and just for him, Emerson wiggled her butt.

When she turned to give him a cheeky grin, Bash was adjusting an obvious erection. "Boner," he said, completely unabashed.

"Are you sure you don't want me to carry

145

any of those," she asked Audrey, who was walking along the thin trail in front of her now. Her back was packed down with bag chairs, and she held her heavy tote as well.

"Nah, I'm good. Shifter muscles," she said over her shoulder with a wink.

Right. Emerson kept forgetting Audrey was probably one-hundred-forty-seven times stronger than her because of the freaking *white tiger* that dwelled in her middle.

Emerson could hear Bear Trap Falls long before she first laid eyes on it. The *rush rush* of the waterfall hitting the river below got louder with every minute of hiking, and eventually, she could smell the mist, too. Evening sunlight sprinkled the forest floor with gold, and branch shadows stretched across the trail, creating beautiful webs everywhere she stepped. The air was crisper up in these mountains, cleaner smelling than down in Saratoga, with a hint of pine sap and rich earth. But it was her first glimpse of Bear Trap Falls that had her slowing to a stop in awe. The banks on both sides of the river were sandy, like beaches, and beyond each were moss-covered rocks and giant fern-like plants that painted the landscape a jungle green. The waterfall itself wasn't too tall, and there was a trail up the rocky cliff that said someone didn't mind jumping from midway.

Bash's hand slid around her from behind, cupping her stomach. He leaned down and murmured against her ear, "This side is Boarlander territory, and across the river, that's Gray Back land."

"Bash, this place is beautiful."

"You like it?"

"Very much."

"Okay, turn around and look up."

She did as he said and looked up into the creaking evergreen branches of the trees that lined the bank. Across several large trees was tied a hand-painted sign that read *Happy Baby Making Day*. The grin that stretched her face felt good. "It's perfect."

Bash hooked a finger under her chin and lifted her lips to meet his. His mouth went soft against hers, and he sucked her bottom lip gently, dumping desire between her legs. With a little moan, she ended the kiss and closed her eyes in an attempt to slow her pulse. In a barely audible whisper, she asked, "Maybe tonight, can you stay in ten-ten with me?"

Bash's smile dipped from his face, then came back slow as he stared at her like he'd never seen anything more beautiful. "I want that." He clapped a hand on his leg and pointed his index finger at her. "First I need to feed you and give you the best night. I brought wine for you. Three boxes. Red, white, and pink. But then I remembered"—his eyes darted to the other Boarlanders who were firing up the grill and setting up the bag chairs on the beach— "we're trying for a cub so I brought you some fruity strawberry-mango juice Audrey likes. It don't have a single drop of alcohol." He shot the others a look again and pressed his hand lightly to her stomach. "Even if it takes us a hundred years to get pregnant, I'll take care of you." He lifted her hand to his lips and smiled through the kiss he laid on her knuckles. Then he made his way toward the grill and settled the giant cooler in the sand.

And her heartbeat raced on.

Five minutes later, Emerson was sitting in a chair, red plastic cup of juice in her hand and tank top stripped off. The sun was hitting her skin just right to get a little tan before it set. Audrey sat beside her and admitted, "I may or may not have cut up cucumbers for us to put on our eyes. I have no idea what that's supposed to do, but I saw it in a magazine, and the boys just laughed at me when I tried it with them. Well, all but Bash, but he ate all the cucumbers."

Emerson laughed and squinted at Bash, who stood with a beer in one hand and a pair of tongs in his other as he settled food on the giant grill someone had dragged out here. "That doesn't surprise me. I'll do it."

"Yes," Audrey said with a little fist pump. She dragged a plastic baggie of sliced cucumbers from her tote bag and handed her a couple.

Emerson stretched her legs out, heals on the sand, as she relaxed back into the chair and settled the green, soothing circles over her closed eyes.

"Thank God," Kirk said from right beside her. "I'm glad she has someone to do girly shit with. Audrey tried to paint my nails last week."

"I did not! I wanted to try one line of color on one fingernail so I could see if I liked it better than the one I was wearing, and you pitched the biggest tantrum."

Emerson stifled her laughter so she wouldn't dislodge her face-fruit. Carefully, she pulled her cup out of the holder on her arm rest and took a long sip.

"It's good you have another girl around here," Mason said in a somber tone. "You deserve to build some healthy relationships."

"Mason, Diem turned out fine. Stop feeling guilty about that."

"Who is Diem?" Emerson asked.

Audrey explained, "Mason used to be the driver slash bodyguard for Damon, the last immortal dragon. Or at least, he was the last one until he gave up his mortality for his mate, Clara...anyway, long story. So he raised his dragon shifter daughter in solitude, and Mason helped."

"Helped keep her in solitude?"

"Yeah," Mason gritted out. "It wasn't my favorite part of the job. New subject. Babies. So you didn't have fake sex in the doctor's office today?"

Emerson choked on the drink she was sipping, and her cucumbers fell off. When she could speak again without wheezing and coughing, she carefully told the shirtless boar shifter who sat in the sand in front of her, "No. I didn't have fake sex." She'd had real sex with Bash.

"Nards had babies," Bash said helpfully.

"Really?" Mason asked.

"Yeah, three of them," Audrey said.

"I call one," Mason said quick.

"Man, what are you going to do with a baby mouse?" Harrison asked from beside the grill.

"Put it in my trailer."

Harrison rubbed his eyes with the heels of his palms and groaned. "Sounds great. We'll just get overrun with mice in every single trailer."

"Nards Junior," Bash said happily. "I want a magic mouse, too."

Harrison's eyebrows arched up so high he made forehead wrinkles. "They shit little chocolate droppings everywhere."

"You call them droppings," Bash said, flipping over a steak. "I call them presents."

Harrison growled and opened the cooler, then pulled out a beer and popped the top. And then he chugged it. Audrey looked at Emerson and made a *ha-ha* face, so Emerson took a sip of her juice to hide her grin.

"Oh, I almost forgot." Bash pulled a plastic container of fruit salad from the cooler and offered it to Emerson. "I packed girl food."

"Bash, that isn't girl food," Audrey muttered as she snatched it from him and wrestled the top off. "It's just healthy food."

"It ain't meat," Bash said. "How healthy can it be?" He took a draw of his beer and looked pointedly at Audrey as though he'd won that argument by a landslide.

With his back to them as he manned the grill, Bash lifted the metal tongs and clicked them once. "Poop Chute Clinton is here."

"Stop calling me that, asshole," Clinton said as he appeared out of the woods.

"I'm making you a steak, Clinton," Bash said, ignoring his vitriol. "It's small and shaped like an anus."

"You guys make me so tired," Harrison said. "No fighting tonight."

"What about arguing?" Clinton asked.

"No, because there ain't no difference in this crew. Arguing always turns to fighting. Why don't you just shock us all and get along with everyone instead?"

"I'm trying to save your lives."

Kirk snorted. "With abstinence?"

"I have in my hands proof that Emerson Elliot," he said, pointing a stack of papers at her, "is an anti-shifter traitor right here in our midst. That's right. I Internet searched you."

Harrison narrowed his eyes and asked in a dangerous voice, "What are you talking about?"

Bash abandoned the smoking grill and placed himself between Clinton and Emerson. "Careful, Clinton," he warned, and now his voice was too low and growly to be mistaken for human.

A chill snaked up her spine as she stood slowly from her chair. "I'm pro-shifter."

"Except for the fact that you edit newspaper articles for the *Saratoga Hometown News*, and your name is on a bunch of openly anti-shifter propaganda pieces."

"Oh." She rolled her eyes heavenward in relief and huffed a laugh. But when she looked around, everyone was staring at her like they'd never seen her before. "That can be explained. I'm a freelance editor, and I don't get to pick my articles. I've edited hundreds of them. I wish I could pick and choose, but they pay me to stay neutral."

"Neutral?" Clinton barked out, squeezing the stack of papers in his angry grip and shaking them in the air. "Quote from the article that released *this morning* on page four. 'The shifters of Damon's mountains should be taken seriously as a threat.'"

"Yeah, and what it said before I edited that sentence was, 'The shifters of Damon's mountains are bloodletting monsters who pose a serious threat to human children.'" She arched her eyebrows. "I've taken the sting off every one of that writer's articles. And besides, I probably have a message on my cell phone right now telling me I'm fired for what I did to that article."

Clinton's furious grimace faltered. "Why?"

"Because read the author's name, Clinton. His real name is Bartleby."

Clinton squinted at the small type on the top page.

"Well, what does it say?" Audrey asked.

"Fartleby."

Bash laughed loud and, beside her, Audrey peeled into giggles and kicked her heels in the sand. Kirk snorted. Mason wore a big grin, looking from Clinton to Emerson to Clinton again. Even Harrison was finally smiling.

"Okay," Clinton conceded. "That's kind of awesome."

Bash leaned down, still chuckling, and kissed her. As he made his way back to the grill, shaking his head, he murmured, "Funny mate."

"Don't call her that," Clinton said, sitting in the chair next to Emerson. He glared at her. "There's still time to get out of this."

"Clinton, if you don't back off, I'm going to drown you in the falls," Bash said over his shoulder. His eyes were glowing green. "I called her my mate because she is."

Clinton dragged his narrowed gaze to

Emerson.

"Sorry, old chap, but it's true. I'm in his life to stay."

"He didn't bite you," Clinton said. "You don't smell like a bear, so I know you don't have a claiming mark."

Emerson strangled her plastic cup. It cracked down the side, and juice leaked out onto her legs. "Maybe someday he'll claim me, or maybe I'll choose to stay human and we'll just get married instead. Either way, what we are to each other doesn't have anything to do with you."

"The hell it does!"

"Emerson and I are trying for a cub," Bash said from right behind her.

She startled at how fast he'd gotten to her, and the look on Clinton's face was nothing shy of terrifying.

"No, she wants artificial insemination from some human she found on the Internet. That's what you said," Clinton gritted out through clenched teeth. Oh, now he sounded snarly, and the fine hairs on Emerson's body lifted.

"She changed her mind. She picked me instead."

"Bash, are you serious?" Audrey asked, sounding shocked. "You're gonna have a cub?"

155

"Get away from her," Bash rumbled to Clinton. "Now."

The air was so heavy it was impossible to breathe, or even move. Emerson was trapped, frozen under Clinton's furious gaze.

"Clinton, move," Harrison said, his words sparking with a power Emerson hadn't ever felt before.

"I'm not gonna hurt her," Clinton said low.

Bash said, "You smell like a fucking bear, and you're too close to my mate. She don't heal like us, fuckwad. Move."

Emerson couldn't breathe. She was suffocating!

Something enormous brushed her arm, and when she dragged her terrified gaze downward, a massive white tiger rubbed her body against Emerson's legs with a loud purring sound rattling the air. When the big cat turned to rub her other side against Emerson's locked legs, Audrey opened her mouth, exposed horrifyingly long canines, and roared at Clinton. Then, panting, Audrey rubbed across Emerson's legs again, just about knocking her over with the affection.

Clinton shook his head and looked like he hated everything, then stood up and made his way to the grill. With one defiant look over his shoulder at Bash, Clinton took something off the top rack of the grill and dropped it in the sand. A pizza roll with tomato sauce oozing out the side of it.

"Oooh, you touched Bash's pizza rolls," Kirk said. "He's gonna kill you, and then Audrey is going to eat you, and then she'll puke you out like a hairball, and then I'll throw you off the side of a mountain, and then Damon will torch you, and then—"

"That's good, Kirk," Harrison said tiredly.

But Bash fist-bumped Kirk and told him, "I like your stories." And then like Clinton hadn't thrown a tantrum at all and Audrey wasn't rubbing all over Emerson like a giant, lethal housecat, Bash grandly announced, "The steaks are done!"

THIRTEEN

"I can't wait until you have a cub," Audrey said over the sound of the water tumbling off the cliff above and into the waves.

Emerson readjusted her backside on the slippery rock under the falls. It was darker here than on the other side, and they'd had to swim deep under the running water to get here, but damn, it was cool in the cave-like space. "I can't wait either. I've wanted to be a mom for so long."

"How long?"

"Since my early twenties. I used to beg my mom to have more babies."

"Were you the youngest?" Audrey asked.

"No, but my sister hit age three and wanted nothing to do with me coddling her."

"I was an only child. Some people like being the only kid, but I didn't. I wanted lots of

158

brothers and sisters."

"I want ten cubs," Bash said from where he bobbed in the water, his shoulders under Emerson's calves.

"Bash, she ain't poopin' out ten cubs," Audrey said, her southern twang thickening.

Emerson laughed and ducked her chin to her chest to hide her flushing cheeks. "I maybe want three."

"Three is good. Or four," Bash said. "Or seven."

Audrey rolled her eyes. "Oh, good God, you're incorrigible. I bet it will be different when you actually have the cub and realize how much work they are."

"Or having one will make me want twenty," Bash said, then pressed a kiss on the inside of Emerson's knee. "Twenty little Emerson's. I hope we have all girls with curly hair and cheetah eyes."

Clinton popped out of the water right beside Bash, and Emerson startled hard. He pushed himself onto the sitting rock and scooted over until his arm touched hers.

"That's close enough," Bash said, void of the humor that had been in his tone a second ago.

"Harrison ordered me to apologize."

Emerson waited for a while, but Clinton just stared at the underside of the falls.

"And?" Audrey said so loud her voice echoed.

"And that's it," Clinton said, casting his Second a dirty look.

Audrey sighed and mumbled something that sounded suspiciously like, "You make me want to take a nap," but Emerson could've been wrong on account of the water being so loud.

"Uh, you're forgiven," Emerson said, desperate to avoid another row with the resident bad bear.

"We need to invent a way of getting booze under here without everything getting wet," Kirk said thoughtfully from his perch on the giant rock behind them.

"Have floating coolers already been invented?" Mason asked. "Or we could try to float Big Blue in an inner tube."

"You named the cooler Big Blue?" Emerson asked.

Mason smirked and nodded like it was the greatest name ever thought up.

"I named my pet plant Spartacus."

"Of course you have a pet plant," Clinton muttered. "You probably have a hundred cats and knit sweaters for them, too."

"I knitted a potholder once," she admitted, unoffended. "Well, I meant for it to be a scarf, but I sucked at knitting so I quit when it was just a purple square."

"I like purple squares," Bash said.

Leaning forward, Emerson ruffled his black hair, dislodging water drops everywhere. "Well, I like *you*."

"Barf and yak," Clinton said.

"Oh, come on, Clinton," Emerson drawled out, resting back on her locked arms. "Haven't you ever had someone you loved?"

Clinton cast her a long, calculating glance. She thought he would say something sarcastic and rude, but instead he murmured, "Yeah. But I destroy the things I love the most."

Pain slashed through her chest at the load Clinton was obviously carrying. But when she tried to ask what had happened to him, Clinton stood and dove gracefully into the water and disappeared under the falls.

Bash gave her a troubled look and lifted one shoulder in a shrug at her questioning expression. "He don't share his story. Not even Harrison knows." He inhaled deeply and curved his lips up in a smile. "Come on. I promised to show you why orange is my favorite color."

Kirk, Audrey, and Mason were now discussing potential names for the baby mice, so she waved at them in a silent goodbye so she wouldn't interrupt. Though she really hoped they weren't being serious about Countess Florence Alligator Razor Teats the First—Teats for short.

Grimacing, she slipped into the cool water and into Bash's waiting arms. He swam them in a slow circle, right on the edge of the falls, and smiled through the mist at her. He looked so damned perfect, his ink-black hair dripping, his eyes the color of moss, the dark stubble on his jaw and that breathtaking smile of his. And he was hers.

"You look all happy right now," he said.

"That's because I am."

He canted his head, and the smile dipped from his lips. Seriously, he said, "Good. When you're happy, it makes it easy for me to breathe."

He pulled her close and kissed her quick, then said, "Race ya." Bash slipped from her arms and disappeared under the dark water.

Emerson sucked in a giant gulp of air and dove down deep. Underwater, she eased her eyes open, and she could see him—Bash. Her mate was swimming with powerful strokes away from her, illuminated by sunrays that broke the surface of the waves. She could see the uneven skin of his burned back, but in this moment, she thought no one else had looked better and more stunning than Bash did here. Arching his back, he swam up to the surface, and she followed.

On shore, Harrison and Clinton were packing up everything, but Bash didn't seem inclined to land there. Instead, he led her farther down the currents and helped her toward the sandy beach thirty yards upriver. She laughed as their feet dragged through the final waves, and with a rush of excitement, she jumped up and clung to his shoulders, then nipped his bottom lip.

"Bitey mate," he mused, then grazed his teeth against her lips as he kissed her. Easing back, he murmured, "Hurry now before we miss it." He grabbed her hand and dragged her up the beach. He didn't slow until they came to a pair of trees, all wound together like they'd grown from the same roots. Bash pointed to a shallow valley between two mountains in the distance and said, "Look there, Emerson."

The sun was sitting right between them, half hidden already. Behind it, the sky was painted in pinks, but the setting sun was a bright and vibrant orange. Emerson gasped at how beautiful it was.

Bash stood behind her and wrapped his arms around her, rested his cheek on the side of her head as the sun sank lower and lower between the mountains.

"Bash?" she asked.

"Mmm?"

She cuddled back against him and whispered so she wouldn't ruin the magic of this moment. "This is my favorite place to be in the whole world."

She could feel his slow smile against her hair. "My favorite place is wherever you are."

FOURTEEN

"Today has been the best day of my life," Bash said, his expression completely honest and open. The glow of the draped outdoor lights around Boarland Mobile Park lit half his face in a soft, gold glow.

She smiled back at him and pulled his hand into her lap. They kept rocking on the chairs on his front porch. "It was my best day, too."

She was still sandy from swimming, but Bash hadn't seemed in a rush to go inside and clean up. He'd stopped here, and really, it was the perfect ending to the night. Bash's face faltered a little, and he spread his fingers out over her stomach. "Emerson, I don't want you to get fired for defending me. You like your job too much. I don't want you unhappy."

She had, in fact, been avoiding checking

her cell phone all day because there was a hundred percent chance Fartleby was pitching a fit over the name snafu and her boss, Margee, had probably left Emerson a bunch of messages. Usually she was totally responsible about returning calls, but today, she'd just wanted to have all the happy moments she could with Bash. She would get the "you're fired" messages tomorrow. Sitting here, looking into Bash's worried eyes with his fingers drawing soothing circles onto her stomach, she couldn't muster the energy to delve into work stuff today.

"I have more newspapers and online venues I freelance for, and besides, I have a backup plan."

"You're sure?"

"Yes. I've never felt surer in my life."

"Are you hungry? Or tired or cold or thirsty?"

She inhaled a breath of crisp mountain air and relaxed into the rocking chair. "I have everything I need right now." She intertwined her fingers with Bash's. Every single thing.

The trailer park was quiet, but not the lack-of-noise kind. More like peaceful. Lightning bugs blinked in the woods behind the trailers, and the windows of Mason and

Harrison's homes were lit. Clinton was off in the woods somewhere, and strangely, this place felt odd without his snarky remarks echoing down the gravel road. Straight across the street, Mason sat against the rails of his porch, one leg outstretched, one bent as he plucked the strings of an old guitar with soft notes that carried this way and that on the breeze.

"I don't want to go back to Saratoga tomorrow," she admitted. "I mean, I know I have to because my computer is there and I need to sort out some messes, but it's nice to imagine just staying here."

Bash lifted her hand to his lips and bit her gently, right between her finger and thumb. "Maybe someday you can stay here. If you want. I don't want to go to work tomorrow. Don't want to miss time with you before you go."

"What time do you leave for your shift?"

Bash scratched his sexy, dark facial scruff with the back of his thumbnail and arched his eyebrows at her. "Six."

"Whoa, that's freaking *early*, Bash Bear. I usually roll out of bed at nine and don't change out of my pajamas until after a few hours of work."

167

"Are you grumpy in the mornings?"

"Not if I have a cup of coffee."

"Then I'll make you a cup of coffee. Breakfast, too, if you wake up early with me so I can see you before I work."

"I'll require bacon for that."

"Done." Bash rocked upward and offered his hand, palm up. "Come on. I want to watch TV with you and pretend we'll do that every night like one of them married couples."

With a grin, she slid her palm against his and reveled in the warm sensation that sparked through her nerve endings where their skin touched. She'd never felt such a connection with another person in her life. And as they walked down the road toward 1010, she realized it had started even before he'd sat down with her at the diner. Her adoration had started with that sweet compliment at the library, and her devotion had begun to grow before she'd even gotten to know the real Sebastian Kane. With every moment she spent with him, he felt more like home.

With a smile, she waved goodnight to Mason, who nodded his chin and kept strumming that guitar of his. Usually, she was a night owl, but she understood the need for the trailer park to go quiet early. Harrison had explained to her they hadn't been hitting their numbers in months thanks to Clinton chasing off most of the Boarlanders. All that was left was this skeleton crew, and they had to endure constant pressure to clear entire mountainsides so the Ashe Crew and the Gray Back Crew could come in with the big machinery and clean the felled lumber for transport to Kong's sawmill in Saratoga. Here was a group of shifters who worked back-breaking manual labor to earn their wages. Her respect for this crew grew with every new thing she learned about them.

"Can I come watch you work someday?" she asked.

A soft rumble sounded from Bash, so she bumped his shoulder and held his hand. "What's wrong?"

"I don't like the thought of you up there. It's dangerous. It would be different if I bit you and put a bear in you, but you're human. You don't heal like me. If something happens to you... I wouldn't be able to work with you up on the jobsite. I'd just hover around you all day. Audrey said girls don't like that shit. I don't want to chase you away."

"It's okay," she murmured, "I understand."

169

She liked that Bash was protective without being controlling.

Inside 1010, Bash started digging around in the pantry, so she said, "I'm going to take a shower and get ready for bed."

"Okay," he said breathlessly as he stared at her with wide eyes.

With a shy smile, she asked, "Dooo you want to take a shower with me?"

Bash answered by stripping out of his T-shirt and speed-walking past her and into the bathroom, stomping across the floor as he went. He left perfect dusty boot prints in a straight line from her to the bathroom that glowed invitingly from the lights above the sink. The tap water turned on.

With a giggle, she pressed her flip-flop in the center of his huge boot print and marveled at the size difference. When she looked up, Bash was naked and frozen, head cocked as he watched her, his lips curved up in a questioning smile. Her heart fluttered in her chest.

How did anyone have the right to be this happy?

She lengthened her stride and stepped into each of his boot prints until she made it to the bathroom. He reached for her so fast his arms blurred, but he stilled just an inch from her skin. After a moment of hesitation, he slowed down and plucked the string of her bikini from behind her neck and whispered, "Gentle." He undressed her slowly with steady fingers, gaze drifting from her eyes to her curvy parts as he pulled the fabric away. "I can't believe you're mine."

Silly bear. He stood in front of her, tall enough to almost touch the ceiling, shoulders wide and strong, muscles cut in defined curves, eight-pack flexing with every breath and those bright, inhuman green eyes looking at her like she was prettier than that sunset he'd shared with her.

Bash turned and pulled the shower curtain back, then offered his hand like she was his queen and helped her under the steaming shower water. He stepped in with her and closed the curtain, casting them in shadow. Emerson had unpacked all her smelly-good toiletries earlier, and Bash watched her with open curiosity as she primped, shampooed, conditioned, shaved her legs, and washed.

Bash sniffed each bottle she used like he was committing her routine to memory. "Girls sure have to do a lot when they shower," he said with a slight frown. "That don't really seem fair. All I gotta do is shampoo and soap. Two minutes, and I'm done, but this is like a part-time job, bein' a girl."

"Well, if you want my legs smooth and me smelling like a botanical garden, this is what has to happen."

"One, I like your natural smell, and two, smooth legs or Sasquatch legs, I'd still do you."

She snorted and closed her eyes against the laugh that lodged in her throat. Dear goodness, she loved the way he expressed his thoughts, so honest and abrupt. She was pretty sure none of her other boyfriends would've given her open encouragement to stop shaving her legs, but that was just Bash's way. He was telling her he liked her however she wanted to be.

Bash took his turn under the water and, sure enough, two minutes later, he was clean and smelling like soap. His back was to her as he rinsed out his hair, and she couldn't stifle the urge to touch the uneven skin there. "Will you tell me what happened?"

Bash tensed under her touch, then slowly he locked his arms against the wall and sighed. "Do you have to know?"

"I would like to so I don't imagine it worse than what it was."

"You can't."

"I can't what?"

Bash turned slowly, and his eyes were so light green it was hard to hold his gaze. "You can't imagine it worse than it was. Harrison's bear ain't right. His dad used to beat him silly, and he can't feel safe. Before Audrey came along, he used to constantly patrol the border of Boarlander territory, just making sure all was well. All day, during his shifts, all night, when he was supposed to be sleeping. I always woke up, too, and waited on my porch at night until he came home. Had to make sure he was okay. And for a while, he seemed like he was getting better. He was patrolling less. But then one day he just took off, tearing out of the trailer park, no warning. He Changed into his bear before he even hit the tree line, but me and the other boys didn't hear anything wrong. Didn't feel anything wrong, and sometimes it was like that for Harrison. Just fast. Uncontrolled. But then I heard it." Bash swallowed hard.

Bash wouldn't look at her anymore, so she hugged him around his waist and rested her cheek against his chest. "Heard what?"

"Gunshots. Poachers had come looking to shoot shifters. People had paid a guide a lot of money to take us, and Harrison gave him an easy target trying to keep them from the trailer park. And Georgia was there."

"Who's Georgia?"

"She's a Gray Back park ranger. Jason's mate. Damon hired her to help take care of his mountains. She got all shot up, too, and I was running as fast as I could, trying to get to them. The boys were following, but Harrison was..." Bash's voice cracked, and he cleared his throat before he continued. "Harrison is my best friend. Mine to protect. I reached him as Damon brought war to those sonofabitches. He was raining dragon's fire, and he's ancient. Good aim, but his fire is wide, and we were all clumped together. I had to protect Harrison. He was bleeding so bad, his fur all matted, and was draggin' himself across the ground, trying to reach Georgia. And all I had time to do was throw myself over him. I caught the edge of the fire, and it was fast. Damon wasn't aiming for me. He was trying to get the men shooting. Trying to protect us. Trying to get us to live. And when it was done, I couldn't see straight I hurt so bad. I didn't want to look because I thought my skin wasn't there anymore, so I just went to work trying to get the bullets out of Harrison so he could maybe heal. Red up to my elbows," Bash murmured in a faraway voice as he rocked Emerson gently from side to side. "He kept saying, 'she saved me,' and Jason was trying to bring Georgia back. The Gray Backs were yelling at her to breathe, and I was trying to stop the red on Harrison. There was fire all around. Ashes and smoke. After that, Harrison had a hard time healing, and things got bad for the Boarlanders. He never said not to show my burns, but I don't want them reminding him of that day, so I just keep them covered when I can."

Every word of Bash's story had broken her heart a little more. Thank goodness for the shower. If she cried quietly enough, Bash wouldn't be able to tell. He pet her wet hair and said, "Shhh," soft as a breath, as though he could anyway.

Bash had led a much more complicated life than she'd realized. All the shifters of Damon's mountains had. He'd been through something traumatic but kept his head up and maintained his positive demeanor.

He and his people had been hunted like animals, and he bore the scars of that awful day, yet Bash hadn't let the darkness poison him. There was immeasurable strength in that.

Swallowing a sob, she pushed up on her

toes and kissed him, grateful he was still here, because that day could've ended up so differently. She could've never met him, could've never known what an incredible man he was. Her life would've been darker for never knowing Bash, and she would've never even known it. She would've just lived a half-life, thinking it was good enough.

She eased back and whispered, "I love your scars, Bash Bear. They mean you protected your friend and survived. They mean you're still here. You don't ever have to hide them around me."

Bash searched her eyes, his chest heaving. He cupped the back of her neck, and then his lips crashed onto hers. When his tongue plunged deep into her mouth, she let off a needy sound, deep in her throat as he pushed her back against the wall. She wanted him. Needed him buried deep inside of her to wash away the trill of fear that had come with the realization of how close she'd come to losing him before she'd even met him.

He gripped her waist, harder than his usual gentle touch. She bit his lip in a tease, proof she liked him feral. His skin clamped between her teeth, she gave him a slow, wicked smile as he let off a soft growl. Hers.

Bash was hers, and that included his wild side. His fingers dug harder into her waist, and she rolled her hips against him, pushing her tongue past his lips. When Bash pulled out of their kiss, his eyes were glowing. Beautiful, beastly Bash Bear. His face had twisted into something fearsome and hungry, but Emerson wasn't scared. He was letting her see a side he kept hidden from everyone else. Chills blasted up her skin when he dipped his lips to her neck and sucked hard. She gasped in ecstasy as he pressed her harder against the wall, his long, thick erection pushing against her sex just right. Behind him, the shower steamed, and water drops raced down his taut shoulders. Slowly, firmly, he gripped her hands and dragged them up the wall until they were trapped above her head. Vulnerable. He wanted her vulnerable and trusting right now, and she fucking loved this.

"Bash," she whispered in a pleading voice.

"Say it again," he demanded, spreading her legs farther apart with his knee.

Defiantly, she bit his chest hard enough that he would feel her. She leaned back and lifted her chin, but didn't repeat his name.

His breath was ragged now, and his lips twisted into a slow grin that didn't reach the intensity of his eyes. "I like you bitey, mate, but don't tease me for long. You'll bleed me or keep them teeth to yourself until you're ready."

She dragged her attention along the edge of the burn on his shoulder. "You want more scars?"

"Just one. Yours."

Emerson twitched her gaze to his and whispered again, "Bash."

He rolled his eyes closed, then sighed, and when he looked at her again, they were such a light color he couldn't pass for human if he tried. Sexy, feral Bash Bear.

Easing his hips back, he brushed the head of his cock down her wet folds, then pushed it into her, shallow and teasing. She was trembling now at the urgency of her body to be connected with the man she loved. She rocked her hips, chasing him when he pulled out. His devilish grin was back, and his face looked different now—feral and intense. He thrust into her deeper and captured her lips with his, swallowed down the moan of pleasure she let off. His hands tightened around hers over her head, and he pushed his entire length into her.

Numb. Emerson's legs were going numb

and her skin was on fire, and in her center, there was this ball of heat building to a beautiful blinding sensation. Bash's pace was slow and calculating, made to torture. Made to keep her right on the edge of orgasm. And when she bucked and begged, "Faster," Bash chuckled low and released her hands, then dragged her waist closer until there was no end to his skin and no beginning to hers.

Bash kissed her slowly, smoothly, his lips like water against hers. "I won't bite you," he promised, just like he had the first time they'd been together, as if he needed to remind his bear not to Turn her.

Safe, so safe. She was safe with her Bash Bear.

He slid his shaft deep inside her, his stomach flexing against hers with every graceful movement. He wouldn't bite her, but she'd made no such promises to him. She wanted him to bear her mark. Wanted his skin to tell shifters he was claimed by her. Emerson drew away from his kiss and pressed her lips on his pec, right above his pounding heartbeat. His hand slid up her arm and around the back of her neck, and gently, he drew her closer, encouraging her. Daring her.

With one last smile against his skin, she bit

him hard. Harder. Harder still until she tasted iron, but he held her there like he felt no pain at all. The snarl in his throat sounded possessive as he jerked his hips and thrust into her. With one last effort, she tensed her jaws, then released his torn skin. She watched three rivers of crimson wash down his chest over his perfect, puckered nipple, down the defined crease under his pec as they faded from red to pink under the water. The watered-down bloodstreams ran over the mounds of his flexed abs before they pooled where her and Bash's bodies met. She should feel horrified. She should be mortified by what she'd done to the man she adored, but when she looked into his face, she couldn't muster the regret. He looked so fucking proud of her. His fiery green eyes drank her in as he whispered out the words, "You. Honor. Me."

Her eyes burned with how big this moment had turned out to be. That mark on him felt huge. Bigger than a human marriage contract. Deep down, on an instinctive level, she knew she'd just bound them in ways that would echo through their lives for always. "I love you," she said, her murmur breaking on the emotion. With a kiss laid above the mark she'd made, she whispered, "Mine now."

His, "I love you, too," came out gravelly and low, beautiful. God, what his admission did to her. She wanted to laugh and cry and hug him tight because it was the first time he'd uttered those words. Bash pushed into her again, and now he wasn't teasing. Wasn't drawing them out. His control had slipped, and the growl in his throat had turned rough as tree bark. When he pulled all the way out and slammed into her again, she arched her back against the cold tiles, crying out his name. Bash pumped into her harder, pushing her toward the edge with every graceful stroke into her body. With a gasp, she closed her eyes and let her body take over. No thoughts, or fears, or questions were welcome here now. Only sensation, and Bash knew how to take care of her. He was so big, so thick, but the stretch felt good as he bucked into her faster. His arms wrapped around her back, Bash pulled her tightly against him as he gritted out her name, the last syllable tapering into a snarl.

Emerson was chanting nonsensical sounds now, completely out of control, completely gone, tipping over the edge as the tingling pressure in her middle built to an inferno. The first pounding pulse of her orgasm rocked her from the middle out, and with her, Bash gritted out a helpless groan and froze. His dick swelled and throbbed, and her insides went warm, then cool, then warm again with every burst of release he shot into her. Pulsing, beautiful sensation—sex hadn't ever felt like this, wild but fulfilling, as if something about her life had come full circle.

There was no doubt in her mind her entire life, all of her choices, all of the heartbreak and triumph, had led her to this moment with him. The one. Her Bash. Her mate. Her everything.

She ran her fingernails gently up and down the uneven skin of his back and left sucking kisses on his neck as he emptied himself completely inside of her. Her aftershocks pulsed on and on, matching his. The water went cold against their legs, but she didn't care. Bash didn't seem to mind either since he was massaging the back of her head now, rubbing the scruff of his face gently against her cheek in animalistic affection, coveting her. She wished she could stay here in this moment forever with Bash telling her without words that he loved her. That he adored her, and she was more than enough for him.

"I never said I love you to another girl," he

said low, his lips right near her earlobe.

Emerson hugged his waist and pressed her cheek against his chest. God, what that combination of words meant to her. Hidden between each one was a secret admission.

You are my only.

She brushed her cheek against his, matching his affection, and said softly, "You're my only, too."

FIFTEEN

The last two weeks had been easily the best of her life. Emerson had somehow managed to only get a warning for the editing 'mistake,' and had even been given permission to submit articles. Margee had seemed excited that Emerson was taking initiative to be a voice against anti-shifter propaganda in the paper. She suspected it was from a combination of Margee's belief that shifters deserved a fair shake and her disdain for Bartleby. In fact, Margee hadn't been able to get through the meeting where she was supposed to give Emerson her formal warning without laughing, and she'd bought her a drink at Sammy's Bar afterward.

With that heaviness off Emerson's shoulders, she and Bash had made the effort to see each other every minute they could.

Sometimes he came to Saratoga after a shift, but most of the time, she preferred to go to the trailer park. It felt homier there, and there was more to do. More people to see. Her friends were there. It was endless barbecues, hikes, and swimming at Bear Trap Falls. The trailer park also meant 1010, watching the baby mice grow, and making sure Nards and Nipples had good food to eat. And above all, the trailer park meant Bash could be himself. And damn, she loved when her man let her see the animal side of him. Heavy-footed, beastly-eyed, lumbering, muscled-up, loyal as hell bear shifter with a growl in his throat for every emotion. In town, he had to hide his power, hide his nature, but in the woods of Damon's mountains, he was free to be his perfect self. It made her love the trailer park even more.

Mornings meant breakfast with Bash and sweet kisses before he left with his crew for the landing. Days were spent with him working on the job site and her editing in the comfort of his office or hanging out with Audrey when she had a day off from Moosey's. Evenings were split. Sometimes they spent time with the crew, and sometimes Bash wanted her all to himself. And nights...nights were her favorite time of day because Bash didn't like sleeping away from her. He would get ready for bed, curl her up against his stomach, and talk to her until she fell asleep, warm and safe beside him.

Everything had fallen right into place...

Until today.

Emerson pulled to a stop right before she reached the newly painted Boarland Mobile Park sign and shook her head. She couldn't do this.

Another deep ache took her stomach, and she doubled over, gripping the steering wheel as her eyes burned with tears. She'd done everything right, charted her ovulation down to an exact science with Dr. Mallory, and she and Bash had started trying for a baby right on the day Dr. Mallory had said would be best. But she'd taken multiple pregnancy tests this morning, and they'd all said the same thing. Not pregnant.

Her body was like clockwork, and now, just as she'd feared, her boobs were tender, and she was feeling those deep cramps that said she would start her period any second.

How was she going to tell Bash? He would be wrecked, and she could barely hold her own disappointment at bay. Just the thought of seeing him hurt over her failure felt like lashes against her insides.

Heartbroken, she rested her forehead against the steering wheel of her little silver Toyota Corolla and let off a pitiful sob.

When the passenger side door opened, she jerked back, rushing to wipe the dampness from her cheeks. Clinton sat heavily in the seat beside her and shut the door, successfully locking her inside a tiny car with a maniac. He wore a trucker hat, holey jeans, and a loose tank top that said *My Only Friend Is Beer*. There was a tattoo on his ribcage, exposed under the low-slung arm holes of his shirt. It was two lines of written script font she couldn't read fast enough before he covered it up.

"I'm fixing up my trailer," he said, staring straight out the window.

"Okay," she said, blinking slowly. Today was weird.

He inhaled deeply and set a yellow dandelion flower on her leg. "Bash said girls like flowers. You can stop crying now." He crossed his arms over his chest and cast her a quick glance, then back out the front window.

Emerson picked the tiny flower off her leg and held it up. It still had the milky film on the stem where he'd just plucked it from a weed patch somewhere. She was going to dry it and keep it forever. "Thank you."

"Not that I care, at all, but if you want to...you know...talk, you can say words to me and I won't yell at you."

"But you hate me."

"Chhh," he said, shaking his head. "I never said that."

"But you're always rude."

"I was trying to chase you away."

Well, at least he was honest. Emerson rested back against the chair and stared at the trailer park beyond the sign. "I have to talk to Bash first."

"About how you ain't pregnant?"

She jerked her gaze to him, and Clinton's gray eyes locked slowly onto hers.

"How did you know?"

"I Internet searched it. Been counting down until you could take one of those tests. It's close, and you're in here crying, avoiding the trailer park. I've only seen you speed into here and basically drift your car into the carport behind Bash's when you show up, all excited to see him."

"I let him down—"

"Oh, bullshit. So you didn't get a baby in you immediately. Woman, do you know how many things have to go right in your body and Bash's to make a cub? A million things. You're wanting to make a miracle, but sometimes it don't happen first thing. You didn't let anyone down. You're going through something completely normal and, besides, have you seen the way Bash looks at you? *You*, Emerson. His eyes aren't on your belly or what you can give him. Bash has wanted to find you for a long time. I promise he won't be mad at you." Clinton pressed himself back against his seat and sighed an irritated sound. "You know what he says up on the jobsite when any of us mention babies or when you'll find out? He threatens to pluck our throats from our bodies if we put any pressure on you."

"Ew."

"What I mean is...Bash knows this ain't a sure thing. He's told me a dozen times it could take a hundred years for him to put a baby in you. Which is weird because you two would be excessively old to have a kid at that age, but whatever. Sometimes it's hard for shifters to have kids, just like sometimes it's hard for humans. Give it time. You'll get the cub you're supposed to raise."

Emerson sat there utterly shocked as Clinton shoved the door open and got out.

"Oh," he said, ducking back into the doorway. "If you tell anyone I picked you that flower, I'll plant sticker burrs in Bash's new yard, burn all his pizza rolls, key your car, tell everyone you wet the bed, and I'll spit in every beer you ever drink from here until the day you die." He gave her an empty grin, slammed the car door, and then sauntered under the entrance sign.

Well, okay then. Pursing her lips, Emerson shoved her car into drive and coasted into the park. Clinton was hammering new framework on his trailer when she walked around the front of Bash's house, and when he looked up from his work, she waved. Clinton flipped her off, but at least he did it with a smile, so that was something.

She climbed the porch stairs, and then, stalling, straightened the rocking chairs before making her way into his trailer. Bash had music playing in his office, so he must've been doing finance stuff. He liked to do math to Metallica for some reason. Emerson couldn't help her smile when she saw him, nodding his head to the hard beat, his back to her, sitting in his office chair going over a complicated spreadsheet that he'd probably memorized by now. He was scary good with numbers. Which baffled her for the hundredth time on why he thought he wasn't a smart man. He said things differently, sure, and he wanted simple things out of life, but that didn't have anything to do with his intelligence. Not in her eyes. She hoped their future cub, or cubs if they were lucky, would be like him.

She had to tell him quick so she could stop feeling so queasy.

"Bash Bear?"

He turned in his chair, smile ready on his lips, a baseball cap on backward covering his black hair. The short, dark stubble on his jaw made his green eyes look even more captivating, and today, he was wearing a tight, long-sleeved charcoal shirt that hugged his muscles and stunned her once again that a man like him was interested in making a life with a girl like her.

The smile dipped from his face when he looked in her eyes. "It's okay," he said immediately, "I got you something."

"Bash, I don't want any presents today." *I don't deserve them.*

"I got you flowers because I thought you might be sad about not getting a baby this month."

She frowned as he passed her by and

jogged toward the kitchen. She followed slowly and teared up as he pulled store-bought red roses from the fridge.

"I bought you the fancy ones from a florist in town because it's not your Friday flowers. I also searched the Internet for girl period stuff, and I got you a heating pad, pain killers, and chocolate, but I accidentally ate most of that on the way home. I think there is one piece left."

She huffed a thick, surprised laugh. "You're not mad?"

Bash flinched back as though he'd been punched. "Mad?" He set the flowers down too rough on the counter. One of the petals fell off, but that was just Bash.

He stomped over to her and went soft millimeters before he touched her skin. He brushed his knuckle over the streak of wetness on her cheek, then stared at the smear of moisture on his hand with an upset furrow to his dark brows. "I'm sad you think I would be mad. Even if we never made a baby, you would still be the best part of me. Are you mad at me?"

She slid her arms around his neck. "Of course not."

"Okay, good, because I don't want you to

leave. And now we get to keep trying. We've been having fun trying, right?"

She giggled and nodded. "The most fun."

"This is the exciting part. The *what-if* every month. And having to wait will make it even better when we finally get our cub." Bash hugged her tight and rested his cheek against the top of her head. "My mom and Bill wanted a baby together real bad. *Real* bad. It didn't ever happen for them, but he still touches her butt all the time."

A million pounds of pressure lifted from her chest with the long sigh she let off. She should've known Bash would make her feel better instead of worse. He was a good teammate. A good partner.

"Look," he murmured, easing back to cup her cheeks. "I'll go turn off my computer, we'll go visit Audrey up at Moosey's and eat tons of barbecue, and then we'll come back and fuck like rabbits."

Emerson snorted at the imagery, but gripped his wrists and nodded. "That would make me feel better. So...we're okay?"

Bash looked at her like she was the silliest creature on planet Earth. "No matter what, we're always okay."

SIXTEEN

Bash inhaled deeply, but these weren't his woods. This wasn't Boarlander territory. He looked around to the unfamiliar pines that creaked in the breeze. Something wasn't right. There were strangers in these woods. People. Humans.

Movement to his left drew his attention, and he crouched, ready for a fight, but it was just Harrison. His alpha came to a stop near him but didn't look at Bash. He was pale and shaken, his hair mussed, and his gaze stayed glued to the space between two tree trunks.

"Harrison?" Bash asked as the hairs on the back of his neck rose.

When Harrison dragged his gaze slowly from the woods to Bash, his dark blue eyes looked hollow, empty. Lifeless. "Run, Bash. Run home."

Home? Bash looked around the strange woods. Where was home?

The crack of metal on metal echoed through the woods, and Harrison fell to his knees. He looked down at his torso with sad eyes. His alpha lifted his hands, palms dripping red, as circles of wet crimson spread across his shirt.

"No," Bash said, stumbling toward him. "No, I saved you. I saved you!"

The whoosh of wind nearly flattened him against the ground, and he looked in horror as something massive flew across the sky blocking out the moon and stars. Damon.

"Harrison!" Bash yelled as he bolted for him.

Fire lit up the night sky as Bash threw himself over his alpha's fallen body. The pain of blistering heat was excruciating on his back, and he gritted his teeth against the scream of agony that clawed its way up his throat. He didn't want Harrison to leave this world on the sound of his pain.

But with the ache lifted and his skin cooled, it wasn't Harrison he heard, but soft crying sounds he didn't recognize. When Bash eased up, Emerson lay in his arms, her curls draped across his forearm, her amber eyes wide and frightened as a single tear streamed down the side of her face. So much red on her shirt, spreading everywhere.

In a hoarse whisper, she said, "Bash, they're here."

Bash shot up in bed, his body drenched in sweat and ready for a battle he didn't understand.

"What's wrong?" Emerson asked in the dark, her hand soothing against his back.

"You're breathing. You're breathing," he chanted mindlessly as he patted her body. Touch wasn't enough. He had to see her. Bash bolted for the light switch and slammed it on.

Emerson winced hard and curled in on herself on the bed of 1010. He was sorry for her pain, but he had to make sure. Bash ripped the neck of the black T-shirt he'd given her and checked her chest for bullet holes.

She had frozen, eyes round and locked on him. "Bash, tell me what's wrong."

He dropped the tatters of her sleep shirt and lurched off the bed away from her. Not gentle enough. He could see her chest rising, could see her skin free of blood, but his bear was still roaring inside of him to Change. Outside, the soft bellow of a bear sounded.

Bash bolted for the front door, and behind him, the soft footfall of his mate followed.

"Bash, what's happening?" she asked in a scared voice, but he didn't have any answers for her. He didn't know. Something bad.

He pulled open the door. His heart banged against his chest like a war drum.

Harrison's massive dark-furred grizzly was pacing back and forth across the road, eyes on the woods behind Bash's cabin. Fuck.

"Stay here," Bash said low.

"Why?" Emerson was holding her tattered shirt together as best as she could.

"I'll be back." *If I'm able.* He kissed her forehead and bolted down the stairs just as Harrison made for the woods. Two weeks wasn't enough time with her. Not near enough.

Bash let the snarling bear rip from his body because it wasn't just Harrison and his crew he had to protect now.

He had to keep Emerson safe from whatever waited out in those woods.

****

Emerson gasped as a massive, coal-black grizzly exploded from Bash's body. When a wave of raw power blasted against her skin, she stumbled backward against the side of 1010.

With long, strong strides, Bash followed Harrison's grizzly into the woods.

Something was wrong. Something bad was happening because she hadn't ever seen fire like that in Bash's eyes. Tensed, growling, every muscle rigid as he'd searched her chest for something she didn't understand.

She sprinted into the trailer and pulled on her jeans and tank top that sat in a pile on the dresser. She shoved her feet into a pair of sneakers and didn't even bother to tie the laces before she sprinted out of 1010 and toward Clinton's trailer. She took his porch stairs two at a time and banged on the door.

"What?" Clinton yelled from inside. Even though she'd spent a lot of time here, it hadn't softened him much.

"Something's wrong. Bash needs help."

Without waiting on an answer, she sprinted to Mason's trailer and did the same. Audrey was jogging down the porch stairs of Harrison's trailer, and Kirk was already headed to the trail in the woods where Bash had disappeared.

Audrey let off a pained yell. She hunched into herself, then fell to her knees on the gravel. Emerson ran to help her, but her friend's body blurred and broke, and Audrey's tiger snarled its way out of her in a matter of moments.

Emerson skidded to a stop in the gravel, but Audrey bolted, her giant paws flattening on the road as she ran after Kirk. Audrey looked over her shoulder and slowed down with a short roar.

Okay, she was in this now. Emerson sprinted after Audrey and tried to keep up as the massive white, striped cat weaved this way and that through dark wilderness she could obviously see much better than Emerson could. *Come on, moon. Give me something.*

She blinked hard to try and force her eyes to adjust as Audrey led her deeper and deeper into the Boarlander woods. She could hear it now—voices, just over the sound of Bear Trap Falls. And through the trees, she saw something that made no sense until she hit the edge of the tree line.

A woman and a man, dressed in black with thick bulletproof vests, stood legs locked, handguns pulled, and facing off with the two grizzlies. Harrison paced back and forth from the bank to the tree line since Bash's black grizzly was cutting him off from getting to the intruders.

The man was tall and lanky, his face red to match his shorn hair. He was yelling, "Back the fuck off. We don't want to shoot, but we will!"

The woman was shorter, thin, and one of her arms was covered in an intricate tattoo that stretched to her elbow on one arm. Her hair was short, chin-length, and bleached blond, and as Audrey skidded to a stop on the beach sand in front of her, another woman's voice shouted, "Drop your weapons. Now!"

Emerson stumbled forward and stopped beside Audrey, who crouched and hissed, as if she was about to attack. Without thinking, Emerson clenched the scruff of her neck and said, "No, Audrey. They'll open fire."

Adrenaline had dumped into her system, and her heart was beating so hard her chest hurt. This was her nightmare, seeing the people she'd come to love threatened like this. Behind her, a quick drumming sound echoed through the woods, and now Kirk was here, a massive silverback gorilla walking slowly from the darkness, eyes on the two intruders and his lips curled back to expose impossibly long canines.

There was a woman holding a weapon trained on the couple that Emerson hadn't seen until she cleared the trees. She was curvy, and her sandy-colored hair was wild with curls like her own, but when the woman ghosted her a glance and ordered, "Stay back," her eyes glowed like a demon's. Shifter.

"I'm Georgia of the Gray Backs, ranger and protector of these mountains, and you are trespassing," she gritted out. She cocked her gun and aimed for the woman's head. "Drop your fucking weapons, or you won't live until your next breath."

"I'm Officer Allison Holman and this is my partner Finn Brackeen. We are part of a task force here to extract a human you are holding against her will." She flashed a badge on her hip and aimed her gun at Georgia. "You put your gun down,"—Holman jerked her chin toward Emerson—"and let her go."

Bash roared a furious, deafening sound and turned on the woman, but Emerson bolted and put her hands up in front of him. "No, Bash!" She rounded on the woman and pleaded, "Don't shoot him. Don't shoot any of them. They're my people!"

Holman's face faltered. "Your people?"

"Tell me you aren't here because of Damon," Clinton said from where he leaned against a tree, his eyes glowing silver.

"We're here to extract—"

"Bullshit!" Clinton's voice cracked across the mountains, and he pushed off the tree.

"Emerson, tell them what you are really doing here."

"I'm Bash's mate. I belong with him. With them. I love him," she said, pushing the words desperately past her tightening vocal cords. "I love all of them. I'm not here against my will. Please don't take them away from me. I just found them."

The woman shook her head over and over, confusion washing over her face. "That's not what we've been told."

"By who?" Emerson asked.

"Your friend, Rachel Mallory, turned in a missing person's report this morning. She said you were taken from your home in distress by Sebastian Kane."

"Rachel Mallory is my doctor, not my friend. I haven't seen her in two weeks. And the last time I saw her, I left her clinic upset because she was spewing anti-shifter garbage at me because of my growing relationship with Bash. She gave you wrong information. I'm here because this is exactly where I want to be."

"Drop your weapons," Georgia gritted out.

The redheaded officer shook his head and held his ground. "If we drop them, what will stop you from murdering us? What will keep you from disposing of us just like you did with all those IESA agents?"

"Look around you," Clinton said.

The officers cast their glances to a commotion on the other side of the riverbank. A dark-furred titan grizzly slipped from the woods, and behind him several pairs of eyes glowed and reflected through the trees. Creed was battle ready and so was his crew, which meant Georgia must've sounded the alarm.

"Your little pea shooters won't save you," Clinton said, coming to stand right beside Emerson and Audrey. "Pull that trigger one time, and you'll have every Boarlander and every Gray Back fighting for your jugulars. But we aren't the ones you're really worried about, are we?"

Something huge blocked the sky like an eclipse, and hurricane winds blew the sand around them into tornadoes. Clinton held Emerson up when her legs failed, and then it was gone and the wind settled.

Bash placed himself in front of her, so close she could smell the richness of his fur. His muscular hump stood high above her head, and she was intimidated to stillness with how big he really was.

"Wait a minute, wait a minute," Holman

said soothingly, holding her hands out, gun gone limp. "Call the dragon off. We aren't here to hurt you. We thought we were saving a civilian. We were just supposed to come in quiet—"

"In woods full of shifters," Mason said from behind them. "You thought you would be quieter than us? Too quiet for us to hear or sense? Who are you, and I swear to God, if we hear a lie, you're dead."

"We've been sent here as the point of contact between the rest of the world and these mountains." Holman holstered her gun. "Brackeen, put it away!" she demanded with a quick, fierce glance at her partner. When he did, she continued. "We have two cabins down the hill where humans will have to check in before they come up here from now on."

"That's not right," Emerson argued. "There are human mates up here. Fuck that. We aren't checking in any time we want to come back from a grocery run."

"Not registered mates, but humans who aren't already paired up."

"Why?" Clinton asked. His lips turned up in a cruel smile. "I already know the answer, but I want to hear you tell the rest of my crew."

Officer Holman swallowed hard and

murmured, "Our objective is to keep peace between humans and the shifters of Damon's mountains as changes to the laws surrounding your existence are reviewed and—"

"Tell them!" Clinton yelled.

The blond dropped her gaze to the sand and angled her face away from the anger in Clinton's voice. "We're here to slow the spread of shifters in these mountains."

"I don't understand," Emerson said, shaking her head.

"They're here for population control," a deep, gravelly voice said from the shadows. "They're here to make sure the shifters in my mountains know their lives aren't their own." Damon Daye, the dragon himself, stepped from the shadows, fastening the last button of a crisp white shirt. She'd seen him from a distance in town once, but standing this close to him, the air was too thick to breath. "We registered, just like they wanted us to. We gave them information about ourselves and our whereabouts, and they've been watching us grow. They're here to undermine everything I've built because our happiness threatens the weak-minded."

"Effective immediately," Officer Holman said in a shaking voice, her neck exposed like a smart little human, "no one else will be allowed to register to the crews of your mountains. No more pairings will be recognized in the eyes of the law."

Bash shrank back into his human skin with a grunt. "But, Emerson is mine," he rasped out, his eyes glowing like the Gray Backs' on the other bank. "I love her. She marked me." He gestured to the scar on his chest.

"I'm sorry." At least Holman sounded regretful. "You can't claim her because she's human. If you Turn her now, they'll cage you."

"I wouldn't Turn her unless she asked."

"Even if Emerson Elliot asks you to Turn her, you can't."

"Well...can I marry her?" he asked. "Can Emerson take my last name?"

Officer Holman looked sick as she shook her head, and Emerson's face crumbled as twin tears streamed down her cheeks. No. No, no, no. She dashed away the dampness under her eyes with the back of her hand. "But he's mine," she said in a pitiful voice. "This isn't fair."

"This isn't my doing," Holman said. "You have caught the attention of people who are much higher up than me. We're only here to keep the peace." She pulled a pad of paper from her pocket and scribbled across it.

"What are you doing?" Brackeen asked in a harsh voice.

"Stand down," Holman barked out when he got too close to her. Illuminated by blue moonlight reflecting off the river, the tough-looking woman ripped off the piece of paper and folded it in half, then approached Emerson slowly, exposing her neck to Bash. Holman lifted her eyebrows high and gave Emerson a loaded look she didn't understand. "If you have any questions about changes in the laws, call me on my cell phone. Here." She shoved it in Emerson's palm and backed away. "Or you can come talk to us at our post. We're located right off the main road on the boundary of Damon's land." Holman twitched her gaze to the paper in Emerson's clenched fist, then back to Emerson's face. To the others, she said, "I'm sorry we had to introduce ourselves to all of you like this. We just arrived at our post to a missing person's report and thought Ms. Elliot was in trouble. Damon, we need to set up a meeting—"

"Maybe tomorrow," the dark-headed, silver-eyed dragon shifter ground out. "Tonight my people have been dealt a blow." He leveled the officers with a dead look and said, "Leave now, and next time you enter my land unannounced, it would benefit you to keep your weapons holstered."

"Is that a threat?" Brackeen asked. "Huh?"

Holman grabbed him by his vest and shoved him toward the trees.

"Or else what, *dragon*?" Brackeen shouted over his shoulder.

"Or else he'll chomp your ass," Willa shouted from across the river. "Right Beaston?"

"Chomp," Beaston agreed in a deep, echoing timbre from the shadows of the trees.

Glowing green eyes and a Cheshire cat grin were all Emerson could see of Beaston in the dim light, and another wave of chills blasted up her arms. She didn't even want to know what the Gray Backs meant by that.

Holman looked like she would retch, but instead she murmured, "I'm really sorry," right before she and her partner disappeared into the woods.

Hands shaking, Emerson unfolded the paper and squinted at the dark scrawl across the center of the note. It wasn't Holman's phone number.

Call Cora Keller of the Breck Crew.

SEVENTEEN

"Cora is going to call us back from a burner phone," Harrison muttered as he continued to pace the gravel in front of his trailer.

Bash sat heavily on the porch stairs and pulled Emerson into his lap, apparently as unconcerned with getting dressed as the rest of them. Dicks everywhere, but Emerson didn't have enough mental energy to be embarrassed. Shifters cared nothing for modesty. Even Audrey was tits out right now as she sank down next to Bash. She was crying, so Emerson held her hand.

When Audrey looked up at her with those big brown eyes, she looked so sad. "You won't get to be bound to Bash, and I won't get to be a Boarlander."

"What do you mean?" Emerson asked,

209

sitting up straighter in Bash's lap.

"I haven't registered with them officially yet. We were going to all go to the courthouse and do a big celebration afterward, but now, I'll remain listed as a lone shifter with my old address. Crewless."

"Oh, my gosh," Emerson whispered. She'd only been thinking about how this new rule affected her and Bash, but Audrey and Harrison were being cut deeply, too. She'd waited her whole life to find a crew like this, and now she wouldn't be an official Boarlander.

Harrison looked gut-punched as he approached Audrey. She didn't get up from her seat on the stairs, so he pulled his mate against his leg. Audrey rested her cheek on him and let off the most heartbroken sob.

The phone rang, and Harrison's voice broke as he answered, "Hello?" Clearing his throat, he put it on speaker phone.

"Harrison, I didn't know you were pairing up or I would've talked to you about this as soon as it began happening last night," Cora said. "The government *knows*."

"Knows what?" Mason asked from where he stood leaned against the railing. His eyes were glowing bright blue.

"Look, we could get away with more when they didn't know Damon and Diem existed. And then there were dragon offspring. Diem and Bruiser had one, Creed and Gia had another, and the government was leaving everyone alone because they knew Damon was very old. Ancient. Immortal. Untouchable. They didn't want trouble. That's what kept his mountains safe for you to live however you wanted."

"They found out he lost his immortality," Mason said in a soft, horrified voice.

"Yes," Cora whispered. "They're trying to change laws without votes, calling it a state of emergency and striking fear into the humans with bullshit ads and information. I'm fighting and rallying as best I can, but it's me and my pull against the country. Do you hear what I'm saying to you?"

"We're losing," Harrison murmured. "They're stripping rights."

"They're doing it to keep the number of dragons and other shifters to a small population, and Damon's mountains have become a safe haven for the most dangerous of our kind."

"We aren't dangerous to humans," Kirk gritted out.

BOARLANDER BASH BEAR | T. S. JOYCE

"Says us. With enough negative publicity against shifters, people will begin to believe anything. Listen. I need to keep this brief because it is chaos here with organizing protests and rallies. The Breck Crew is in clean-up mode. You have two females now, right?"

"Yes," Harrison and Bash said at the same time.

"If you want anything done, we have delayed the changes until noon tomorrow. I hope to God we can get everything overturned, but I don't know how much time it will take or if we'll ever get these rights back. If you want anyone bound to the Boarlanders, you have until midday tomorrow."

"Why didn't those damned officers just say that?" Clinton asked, sounding pissed.

"They weren't supposed to," Emerson said, feeling hollow inside as she lifted the crumpled note. "Holman broke some rule by giving me this information. She was trying to tell us we had a little more time, but her partner wouldn't have been on board with that outright admission."

"My advice, for what it is worth," Cora said in a softer tone. "Pledge or do whatever it is you want to legally do by tomorrow, and then go to work. Build your public relations in Saratoga and beyond, as far as you can reach. We'll be doing the same from Breckenridge. Half-naked lumberjack calendars for woman, interviews, donations, blogs—whatever you can do to show how normal we are to the public, do it. We have a battle ahead to get us back to where we were."

"Okay. Thanks Cora, we'll keep in touch."

"Yep. Good luck tomorrow, and Harrison?"

"Yeah?"

"Whatever you do, don't let Damon eat anyone until this all blows over."

The line went dead, and Harrison looked like he wanted to chuck his phone into the woods. "Like any of us can control that," he gritted out. "Damon only goes all hungry dragon when we're being attacked, shot at, hurt, annihilated. If we don't have his fire, these mountains fall. The Ashe Crew, the Gray Backs, the Boarlanders—we're all sitting ducks."

"No, we're sitting grizzlies, dragons, silverbacks, boars, birds of prey, tigers," Mason ground out. "If they come at us, the shifters here aren't defenseless. I'll talk to Damon about keeping a low profile. In the meantime, we need to worry about tomorrow." He arced his blazing blue gaze to Emerson and Audrey. "If you want legal ties to this crew, now might be your only chance."

EIGHTEEN

Bash had disappeared shortly after the call with Cora Keller. He'd seen Emerson to 1010 and then left without another word. The snarl in his throat was constant, and his eyes glowed like a beast, but the look on his face right before he left said he was just as shattered on the inside as she was.

How was she supposed to sleep after what had happened tonight? She'd tried, but every time she closed her eyes, she saw those guns pointed at Bash's bear, and the flashbacks felt like getting hit by a car.

At five in the morning, she gave up on sleep and made breakfast, sure that he would come in from his Change, or whatever he was doing, but instead, she sat at the table with two plates of food that eventually went cold. She couldn't even stomach a single bite.

Everything had gotten so messed up in such a short time that her head was spinning.

Giving up on him coming back, she dressed and readied for the day, then struck out on her own to find him. She'd never seen Bash down, and she had no idea how he handled heartache, but she knew one thing. Neither one of them should go through this alone.

Emerson didn't know how she knew where he was, but some long buried instinct must've kicked up in light of almost losing her mate last night. Maybe she was still losing him, she didn't know. Bash had wanted a mate, claimed or married he hadn't minded either way, but he wanted to be bound to a woman, and now that wouldn't be possible for them.

She stumbled through the woods in the early morning light, her hiking boots squishing against the soft ground. Dew clung to everything and quieted her normally clumsy footsteps. Bash wasn't right under Bear Trap Falls, but she hadn't expected him to be. She was looking for a special place. The orange place.

Emerson made her way up the beach, her shoes sinking deep into the sand with every step, but when she did see him, she stuttered to a stop. He sat on a bench in front of the two intertwined trees, elbows resting on his knees, shoulders hunched as he looked at something in his hand. He closed his eyes, clenched his fist, and let off a long exhale, then he slid his troubled gaze to her. His eyes were still the unnatural green that said his bear hadn't settled.

After a slow approach, she sank down onto the bench beside him. It smelled like sawdust and new stain, and on a plaque nailed to the backrest, it read, *Emerson's Favorite Place*.

Her lip trembled, and she slid her hand into the crook of his elbow. She stared over the river at the mountains. "Did you build this for me?"

Bash swallowed hard and wouldn't meet her gaze. "I got you two presents for yesterday. The flowers and the period stuff if you weren't pregnant, and this if you were."

She stared at the woodgrain and the rich, dark color of the finely made wooden bench and shook her head, baffled. "I don't understand."

"Not the bench." Bash unclenched his hand, and on his calloused palm sat a sparkling antique diamond ring. The main jewel was round and brilliant, but the setting had smaller, intricate diamonds all around that tapered into a thin band.

"Bash," she said on a breath.

"Don't. Not yet. I know your answer. I just wanted to tell you what I had planned before everything got so fucked up. I bought a ring before I met you. I was on the hunt for a mate, and I was ready for commitment. Platinum. Two carats. Gaudy as hell, but I thought I would have to put a fancy ring on a woman's finger if she was gonna marry a man like me. But then I met you, and that ring didn't feel right. It wasn't you. It was big and flashy, but you're a classy, quiet, understated lady. You want simple things, like me. So I got this one. I showed it to Audrey, but she told me the same thing she always does."

"Slow, Bash," Emerson whispered, blinking hard.

"Yeah. I'm ready. I was ready that night at Sammy's Bar. You're mine, and it don't make no matter to me whether we get married today or ten years from now—I'm in this. But you're human, and time moves different for your kind."

"Bash, *you* are my kind." She swallowed hard and blew out a steadying breath. "Ask me if you want."

He jerked his wild gaze to her and froze.

She couldn't even tell if he was breathing as the seconds and silence stretched between them. Then slowly, Bash dropped to his knee in the sand. He took her hand in his and offered up the ring between his finger and thumb. "This isn't how I wanted it. I wanted you to be able to plan a big fancy wedding and invite all of Saratoga and have a chocolate fountain and piles of pizza rolls. I wanted to throw a big party and shout to the world that you picked me, but all I can give you is a rushed wedding up at city hall."

"That's not all you have to offer."

He cocked his head and smiled. "Okay, also a shitty trailer in a shithole trailer park and a crazy crew of—"

"Stop it. I'm being serious. What else do you think you have to offer me?"

"My body. I'll always protect you, no matter what. I'll always have your back. I won't make you raise our cubs alone. I'll hold you when you cry and feel damned proud to have you on my arm. I'll never stop trying to make you happy because that smile on your face, the one you're wearin' right now, is the best part of my day. You'll have to deal with all my gritty parts, but you can have all my good parts, too."

She smiled and spread out the fingers of her left hand as her vision blurred with her tears. "That sounds like a damn fine offer to me, Bash Bear."

A slow grin curved his lips. "You mean you'll marry me? Even though you aren't carryin' my cub?"

She swallowed hard over and over so her answer would come out strong. "Of course I will."

Bash squeezed his fingers too tight and the ring popped out of his grip like a firecracker. They both gasped as it hit the sand and disappeared. Frantically, Bash scooped a handful of the dirt and sifted through it. "Too rough," he growled out as he pulled the ring from the pile in his hand.

"Oh, dear goodness, Bash. You nearly gave me a heart attack!" Emerson's heart was lodged somewhere between her collar bones and her throat.

But when Bash looked back up at her, he was grinning so big she laughed. He pulled her hand away from her chest where she'd clutched her shirt when he'd dropped the ring, and he slid it onto her finger.

Bash hugged her up so tight she couldn't breathe, but she didn't care. Yesterday had been the worst day, but today was going to be amazing. Bash was making sure of that.

Face buried against her neck, Bash murmured, "I thought you would say no. I sat here thinking our timing was bad. Bad timing, bad luck, but you said yes. To me." He shook his head against her and hugged her closer. "To me," he repeated softer. He loosened his hold on her, and thank goodness because she was beginning to feel dizzy at the lack of air.

"Let's go tell everyone," he said, his eyes round. His excited smile was breathtaking in the gray morning light.

"I love the bench you made for us to watch the sunsets on. And I love the ring you picked for me. It's perfect—exactly what I would've picked."

"I measured your finger with a string the first night we slept in ten-ten so the store could make the size right. Let's go tell everyone," he said again, more urgently.

Emerson laughed as he dragged her off the bench and pulled her along the beach behind him. "Too slow, human," he finally said when she'd slowed to stare in awe at the ring on her finger. She was really engaged to Bash. She was engaged to the man she'd met years ago who'd paid her a sweet compliment at the library.

Bash turned and folded her into his arms, then strode toward the trail that led to the trailer park. When he started running, she held onto his neck for dear life because her stomach was doing flip flops with how fast he was going.

"Harrison! Kirk! Audrey!" Bash called as they came out of the woods behind his trailer. "Mason!"

"Don't forget Clinton," she reminded him.

"Oh, right. Asshole! I have to tell you something!"

Most of them were already gathered around Harrison's trailer at the front of the park, and Mason stuck his head out of the trailer next to the alpha's as they passed. Emerson flashed her ring at him, and he grinned.

Breathlessly, Bash set her down and told the others, "I did it. I asked her and she said yes and look." He shoved his finger at her ring. "Emerson's gonna be my wife." Quieter, he repeated, "My wife."

Audrey got to him first and hugged him up tight. Emerson couldn't stop laughing and crying and shaking as they embraced her one by one. Clinton kept his distance, but he did pet the top of her head awkwardly like she was a cocker spaniel, and the affection counted. He almost cracked a smile, and she was convinced, deep down, Clinton liked her.

"Okay, if we're gonna do this, we have to go now," Harrison said. "It's a long drive to Saratoga, and we still have to beg, bribe, and bully for a last minute marriage license."

"I have to put on something nice," Audrey said, her voice pitched high with excitement.

"Okay, go get ready, but we're out of here in half an hour," Harrison said. "If you ladies aren't polished by then, you'll have to put your war paint on in the truck."

"Break!" Bash said, clapping loud. "Wait," he called after Emerson as she bolted for 1010.

"Yeah, fiancé?"

"Oh, damn I like the sound of that," he said through a startled grin.

"What were you going to ask me?"

"Oh! What should I wear?"

"You should wear your favorite outfit."

"So...naked," he said with a decisive nod.

"Nope," she said. "You have to wear clothes."

"That was a joke probably," he murmured as he walked toward his trailer.

Audrey caught her hand and tugged her

BOARLANDER BASH BEAR | T. S. JOYCE

toward 1010. "I have to borrow a dress because I don't have any that will work, and you always wear cute shit."

"Okay, but I only have half my sundress stash here—"

"Good enough."

As it turned out, Audrey had much smaller boobs than Emerson, but she happily stuffed her bra and looked like a goddess in her red eyelet sundress. And Emerson felt like a million bucks in her white, strappy beach dress with the gold embroidery along the hem. She wore her favorite pair of strappy, gold sandals with it. And after she stripped the thorns from an Emerson rose from Bash's landscaping, Audrey pinned it into the cascade of curls fastened at the back of her head. She made a matching bouquet, smoked up her eyes, slathered on pink lip glitter and called her look done. Sure, it wasn't the traditional wedding gown she'd dreamed of as a little girl, but the look in Bash's eyes when he laid eyes on her right outside of 1010 made her feel like the most beautiful woman in the world.

Bash opened his mouth to say something as she approached, holding her bouquet of pink roses tied with twine, but he clacked his teeth closed and just shook his head with an awed look instead. He was dashing in his black sweater and dark-wash jeans with his hair all gelled and designer-messy. He'd even shaved so she could see every sharp angle of his chiseled jaw.

He ran his knuckles over her cheek, but it was dry, and when he traced her smiling lips, she understood. She was happiest when he was happy, too. When he cupped her neck and pressed his lips to hers, she relaxed against him. After he eased away, she could see it there in the forest green hue of his eyes. Even without words, she could *see* his love for her. Somehow, despite everything, the fates had known exactly what they were doing. After today, there would be no uncertainty about her future with Bash. No one would be able to keep them apart.

"Come on, love birds," Kirk called from where he was climbing into his green muscle car with Mason and Clinton. "We have to go now."

"Yep," Bash called behind him, seemingly unable to take his eyes off Emerson. "We'll be right behind you."

"Let's go get hitched." Emerson stifled the excited squeal that was bubbling up her throat and pulled Bash's hand toward his carport.

Someone had tied blue beer cans to the bumper. They would probably be destroyed by the time they got to City Hall but at least they were getting that part of the wedding day. She bet it was Kirk.

Bash pulled out onto the gravel road but skidded to a stop when Harrison waved them down. He and Audrey climbed into the back seat, and Bash hit the gas, following the trail of dust Kirk had left behind.

"What if we can't get the marriage license in time?" Emerson asked.

"Mason and Damon are taking care of that. We just have to get there in time to do the paperwork," Harrison murmured, texting furiously on his phone from the back seat.

"What if we don't get there in time?" Emerson asked in a rush. "What if there is a herd of goats in the way, or an avalanche, or—"

"Stooop," Audrey drawled out. "We'll make it."

"I have to call my parents and my sister. You might want to plug your ears if you don't want to hear them screaming."

"With joy?" Audrey asked.

"No." With disappointment and curse words. When she'd told them about Bash, they

226

hadn't been on board. In fact, they'd called this another one of her questionable decisions, but again, it was her life, and if they didn't like it, tough shit. They hadn't liked any of her ex-boyfriends, didn't consider freelance editing a "real job," and hadn't supported her decision to have artificial insemination, so somewhere along the way, Emerson had learned she had to depend on her own opinions to chase her happiness. She loved them, but they were too rigid in their belief of what "normal" was. She would never fit that mold. Emerson slid her hand over Bash's and returned the smile he gave her. Maybe that's why they worked so well. Neither one of them fit a mold. They were two oddly-shaped lumps of clay that somehow fit together to make something great.

With a steadying breath, Emerson pulled her cell phone out of her purse and dialed her parents' landline.

"Hello?" Mom said in a sleepy voice. Oh crap, it was still early in the morning.

"Oh, I'm so sorry I woke you."

"What is it, Emerson? What's wrong?"

"Nothing's wrong. Everything is right. Can you put dad on the phone?"

"Dan," Mom said tiredly. "Dan, wake up. It's Emerson, and she sounds like she's on drugs or something."

On drugs? Audrey snorted from the back seat as if she could hear the muffled conversation. And knowing her heightened shifter abilities, she probably could.

"Emerson?" Dad asked in a hoarse voice.

"Hi, Dad. No, I'm not on drugs. I'm actually calling to tell you I got engaged."

"What?" Mom asked, her voice pitching painfully high.

Emerson winced and pulled the phone from her ear by inches. "Bash asked me to marry him, and I said yes, and before you go crazy, I just want to say I love him, and he is very good to me, and I'm happy." She pulled the phone farther away. "Now you may yell at me."

Dad sighed deeply. "He makes you happy?"

Hope blooming in her chest, Emerson rushed out, "He makes me devastatingly, breathlessly happy, Dad. He's the one. I knew it from the first time I talked to him, and he knew it, too. I want a life with him, a family, the whole nine yards. And I really, really want you to be happy for me."

Mom sniffled. "How did telling us this news make you feel, honey?"

"Scared," she admitted.

"See, that's not what we wanted, and that's our fault for not being more supportive. It's scary to us that you are in love with a shifter, and this all has happened so quickly."

"But when Amanda fell in love and got engaged right away, you were so happy, Mom. You were so excited to plan the wedding, and she was only twenty-one at the time. I'm twenty-eight, and I know Bash is it. I've waited a long time for him. I want you to be happy for me, too. And I want you to come to the wedding."

One of her parents sighed loudly into the phone. "When?"

"Today."

"What?" Mom said, too loud.

"We don't have a choice. The shifters are being stripped of rights, and if Bash and I don't get married before noon today, we won't be allowed to legally wed."

"That's awful. Not the wedding, I mean them not being able to marry."

"Yeah. It was a big blow. My friends...well, it was a really bad night for the shifters in Damon's mountains last night."

"I'm so sorry, honey. I had no idea you were dealing with so much stress. You should be allowed to be with the man you choose, and

229

Dad and I haven't made this any easier on you either. This isn't the wedding I imagined for you, but you're also a grown woman. And Emerson, I haven't heard you this happy in...well...ever. Every call from you over the past couple of weeks has lifted my heart, and if part of that is Bash's doing, well, you have our blessing. Where should we meet you? I can bring something borrowed and blue."

"Saratoga City Hall. We'll be there soon."

"Okay, call your sister and tell her your news. Dad and I will be there."

Emerson wrapped her arms around her middle and swallowed her emotions down. "Really?" she asked in a small voice.

"Of course," Mom murmured, her voice quavering. "We wouldn't miss your big day."

"We love you, honey," Dad said. "We'll see you in a little while."

"I love you, too," she croaked out. "Bye."

She ended the call and stared at her phone. Well, that went about a thousand times better than expected.

Audrey sniffled from the back seat, but Emerson didn't turn around to console her because if she saw her friend crying, she was going to lose it and have smeary-mascara-raccoon-eyes for her wedding. And sure, Bash would probably find a way to make her feel cute anyway, but her future husband was a solid ten on the sex-appeal scale, and she wanted to be in top form next to him for pictures today.

As she looked out the window at the piney woods blurring by, it hit her. She was really getting married today to the man she loved more than anything. She would be surrounded by friends who were happy she would be a part of the Boarlanders now, and her parents would be there as she said her vows, supporting her. There was no more room to worry that something could go wrong because Bash looked calm and collected beside her, and Harrison was in the back seat on his phone purchasing a rush-order wedding cake in the shape of a bear from a local bakery like everything would be okay.

And if her crew—*her crew*—was this confident that today would go off without a hitch, well, it was time she started trusting the fates who had done so well getting her here.

NINETEEN

Emerson was getting *married*. The drive to City Hall had stretched on and on, each minute dragging, but when they'd arrived, it had been chaos. Happy, lovely, beautiful chaos.

All of the things she'd feared never came to fruition, and now she was here, surrounded by the Boarlanders, flanked by Audrey, who was newly registered with the crew, and her parents, who donned smiles on their faces. Emerson was in this incredible moment, looking up into Bash's clear green eyes. She could see her reflection there, from her trembling smile to her tear-streaked cheeks, when she said, "I do."

Bash lifted her up in a bear hug, but the officiant said, "Wait, wait, wait, you're not done yet."

"Oh," Bash said. "I got excited."

With a giggle, Emerson slid back down to the floor and nodded to the officiant.

"I now pronounce you man and wife."

Bash grinned big, his eyebrows arched high, and God, she loved him more than anything.

The officiant dragged it out with a teasing smile, but at last he said, "You may now kiss your bride."

Her new husband came at her fast, but in true Bash fashion slowed just before his lips touched hers. He sipped her softly, his tongue barely brushing the closed seam of her mouth. Gentle bear, but only with her.

He lifted her off the ground to the cheering around them, and she crossed her ankles and hugged him up tight when he ended their kiss. But where she expected him to be smiling when he eased away, her Bash Bear's eyes were rimmed with moisture, and he buried his face against her neck quick. She blinked hard to clear her vision as she looked from Harrison's smile as he whistled long and loud, to Audrey who was wiping her eyes with the back of her hand, to Mason who took pictures with a disposable camera he'd picked up from somewhere, and Kirk, who was clapping, to Clinton, who stood with his hands in his pockets. He nodded to her as though she'd done well. It didn't matter that she hadn't gotten the big wedding she'd thought she wanted as a kid.

There was no way anything could match this moment.

Bash sniffed and set her down, and then Harrison drew him into a manly, back-slapping hug. She hugged her parents, and they were so sweet and supportive, and when it was Audrey's turn to embrace her, she held Emerson for a long time, rocking gently.

"I've always wanted a friend like you," Audrey whispered. "Welcome to the crew."

Emerson squeezed her shoulders and eased back to dab her cheeks with a tissue. The officiant shook her hand and said, "I'm sorry this was rushed. I don't agree with what is happening to you and your people. I wish you a long and happy life with your mate."

And just like that, her disappointment in people vanished. Last night had shaken her to the core. It had made her feel picked on and jaded, but the human officiant and his kind words reminded her that there was more good than bad in this world. That people could be understanding and accepting.

The world just needed to be made aware

that there was no reason to fear shifters. She thanked him and turned to see Bash talking and laughing with her parents. They liked him, she could tell. How could anyone not adore Bash? He was sweet and funny and cared more than anyone she'd ever met. Emerson made her way to him and slipped under his outstretched arm, the grin on her lips feeling permanent. Today had been one of those days that had turned out to be unimaginably happy, and what a way to start their lives together.

Bash kissed the top of her head and told her, "I just invited your parents to the after-party."

"What after-party?" she asked, baffled. She'd figured they would take the cake back up to the trailer park and hopefully order some barbecue from Moosey's. Nothing big or flashy, since this had been about as rushed as it could get.

"It's a surprise."

Her mom was smiling, and her eyes were rimmed with tears, her dad hugging her tight against his side. Amanda hadn't been able to make it last minute, but at least her parents were starting to see the magic of these people. "We'll be right behind you."

"Okay," Emerson said, feeling numb as

Bash ushered her out the double doors behind the rest of the chattering crew.

A short drive later, and Bash parked his pickup in the gravel parking lot of Sammy's Bar. Harrison and Audrey slipped silently out of the truck and shut the door.

"Remember this place?" Bash asked.

"Yeah, this is where you had your Meet-A-Mate Bash."

He leaned over the console and drew her knuckles to his lips. "And I did. You. This was the place I figured out you were mine. My bear picked you here."

There were people piling in through Sammy's doors. She recognized some of them from the crews she'd met over the last couple of weeks. Brooke and Tagan of the Ashe Crew. Kellen, Skyler, Bruiser and Diem, Drew and Riley, and others. Willa and Matt waved before they went in, and Beaston nodded his chin at them as he helped his very pregnant mate, Aviana, through the door to Sammy's.

"But...I thought everyone was working up on the landings today."

"Being C-team paid off. The Ashe Crew and Gray Backs don't have job sites because we're so fuckin' behind cutting their trees. Kirk called Kong and Layla, and they opened the bar early and went to work. Damon gave everyone a day off. They came here for us. For you."

She would *not* cry again, she would *not* cry again. Swallowing hard, she opened the door and slid out of Bash's truck, then took his hand and followed him across the parking lot.

As she stepped inside the bar behind her new husband, Kirk lifted his beer and yelled out, "Mr. and Mrs. Kane of the Boarlanders!"

The bar erupted in applause, ear-splitting whistles, and cheers. It looked like all the crews were here, children and all, like one big family. And in the center of them were Mom and Dad clapping the loudest. Denison Beck got on the mic and lifted a shot glass. It was damn early to be drinking, but that didn't have any bearing on this party. "You all lift your glasses. Last night, we got some rough news, and it was hard, and it hurts. But none of that matters today because Bash married his lady, Audrey registered to the Boarlanders, and today is a great day."

"Hell yeah!" Kong yelled from behind the bar.

Denison laughed with the others and lifted his glass higher. "To Bash and Emerson. Welcome to the family!"

BOARLANDER BASH BEAR | T. S. JOYCE

And as the others drank a toast, Bash dragged her out onto the dance floor and hugged her close. Brighton Beck plucked some slow notes on his old guitar before Denison belted out a first, soulful note. Emerson melted into Bash's embrace as he rocked them back and forth.

The bar was loud, crowded, sticky-floored, and perfect. There was a bear-shaped cake on a table near the stage where a couple of kids were swiping frosting. She thought Willa was going to chase them off, but the spunky redhead only took a swipe of her own and shushed the kids' giggling. Beside Emerson and Bash, Beaston danced with his Aviana, and Mom and Dad were slow dancing near them, too. Today had been beautiful. It had been one of those days that had the potential to make an entire lifetime. It had been a fork in a long road. She'd taken a risk and it had paid off. She'd found the path paved with joy.

"You smell happy," Bash murmured, his cheek against her hair.

"I am. I was really lonely before you, and now look what you've given me."

"Sex and pizza rolls?"

She laughed and shook her head. "Those and so much more."

Bash looked so handsome in the dim lighting of the bar. "Remember that time you told me you like everything about me?"

She slid her hands up his chest, hooked them around the back of his neck and nodded. "It's still true."

"No one ever said that about me before." His lips twitched into a smile, then fell. "I feel like that about you. You make it easy to breath, Emerson. I think you're my air."

She bit her trembling lip and rested her cheek against his chest. "You're my air, too, Bash Bear."

EPILOGUE

In a daze, Emerson emerged from the trailer she shared with Bash and stumbled toward his waiting truck. The last week since the wedding had been complete and utter chaos with trying to get her name changed, her address changed, moving out of her duplex into Bash's trailer, and writing her first article for submission.

In all the commotion, she'd missed something vital. Something amazing.

"Light a fire, woman," Kirk called from the bed of Bash's truck where he had piled in with Mason and Clinton, who was now staring at her with an obnoxious, knowing grin as though he was a damned psychic.

Ignoring them, she crawled into Bash's truck and buckled in. When she turned and met his gaze, his dark brows were furrowed with concern. "What's wrong? Is it Clinton? Do you want me to bleed him?"

"No. No, I'm fine. I'm just...surprised by something and need a minute to think."

"You want music to think to? Heavy metal helps." He turned the knob on his stereo and blasted a heavy beat.

"Ten bucks says Beaston won't even let us hold him," Audrey said from the back seat.

Harrison snorted as Bash pulled out of the trailer park. "He probably doesn't even let Aviana hold him."

Beaston's call that his mate had given birth to their raven boy this morning was what had triggered a series of realizations. After her negative pregnancy tests, Emerson had been sure she would start her period at any moment, but then her life had gone chaotic with the wedding and the aftermath, and she'd forgotten about it completely. But now she was definitely a week late, and the test she'd just taken had two bold lines.

She was pregnant.

Pregnant.

She couldn't help her smile, and her heart pounded against her chest.

The million things that had to come together to make a miracle like Clinton had said...well...she and Bash had done it. Emerson pulled her oversize purse closer against her stomach, now carrying a tiny, fragile life.

She was going to be a mommy, and he was going to be a daddy, and she was utterly overwhelmed with emotion right now.

"You're making the air weird," Bash said suspiciously. "Are you sure you're okay? If you don't want to go see Beaston's baby—"

"No! I really, really want to see his little boy." And cuddle him and smell him and cry over him because she and Bash would be holding their own cub soon.

Bash pulled to a stop at the main road. On the left, in the shadows of the evergreens, sat the new cabins where Holman and Brackeen were posted, an ominous symbol of the changes that were slowly affecting life here. But to the right lay the road to Grayland Mobile Park. And there, cradled in the arms of Beaston, lay something no one could take away from the shifters here. Hope.

The truck tires rattled over the wooden bridge that crossed the river fed by Bear Trap Falls, and gravel kicked up as they blasted down the road and under the Grayland Mobile Park sign.

Bash parked in front of a bricked-in fire

pit, and as a crew, they walked past the other trailers and into the woods where Beaston's house was. His woods were flooded with shifters and humans alike, paying their respect to the newest inhabitant of Damon's mountains.

The dragon himself stood by his mate, Clara, holding his young son and talking quietly with Tagan James, alpha of the Ashe Crew. The crowd parted as Harrison led them up to the trailer, up the porch stairs, and inside.

Beaston and Aviana's house reminded Emerson of the inside of a tree with bark walls and colored cloths over the lamp, muting the light, but their bedroom seemed like a different world. It was simple and clean. Aviana looked beautiful, tired but smiling as she lay under the thick comforter beside her mate. Beaston sat on the edge of the bed, staring at a tiny bundle in his arms.

When he looked up, his glowing green eyes were raw. "He's a raven, just like I dreamed. He's a raven like my Ana."

Harrison cupped the back of his head and pressed his forehead to his, then eased back and squeezed Aviana's hand. "He's a cunning boy."

"I tried to let people hold him. I tried," Beaston said, shaking his head. "I can't. Not yet."

Aviana rubbed his back and looked happy. She was glowing as she watched her boys.

"That's okay," Bash said, stepping closer. "I wouldn't want to let anyone hold my baby either. He has your face. Bright eyes, but he's fine-boned like Aviana. Look at his little fingers. He'll be a good flyer someday. He's perfect, Beaston."

Beaston cast Bash a grateful look and then stood and held him out for everyone to see. "His name is Weston Novak."

Weston to match his father's given name, Easton. Emerson smiled as the baby gripped Beaston's little finger.

Bash had a hard time leaving when Harrison was ready to give Beaston and Aviana some space. She could tell he wanted to look at Weston longer. He would make a good daddy like Beaston.

Outside, the Boarlanders mingled with the other crews who stood around talking, but Emerson took Bash's hand and led him back through the woods to the quiet trailer park.

"I have a present for you," she murmured, resting her hips back against his truck.

He'd gone quiet since they'd left Beaston's house, and now his lost-in-thought look morphed to one of concern. "I didn't know we were supposed to get each other presents today."

"We aren't." She pulled the stuffed teddy bear he'd given her from her purse and handed it to him.

Bash's frown deepened. "I don't understand. Are you giving it back to me?"

"No, Bash," she said with a significant look. "It's for our baby."

He looked from the floppy stuffed bear to her and shook his head in confusion.

With a smile, Emerson pulled his palm to her stomach and held it there, her wedding ring glinting in the sunlight. "I was wrong last week. I think it was too early to test."

Bash's face went slack, but then his eyes pooled with emotion. He straightened his spine, shaking his head in denial. "Don't tease me."

"I'm not. I saved the test at home to show you. Two lines, bold as anything. We're going to have a baby, Bash. You're going to be a daddy."

Bash dragged her to him and hugged her shoulders tight but didn't take his hand away from her stomach. He rocked her back and forth for a long time, just shaking his head and breathing deep. She'd thought he would want to shout it to the crews, but he just stood there, wordless, rubbing his cheek against the top of her head as his body trembled.

In a broken voice, he recited her words from their wedding day. "I was really lonely before you, and now look what you've given me."

When she opened her eyes, the Boarlanders were standing at the edge of the trees, watching them with knowing smiles.

Bash was happy.

Her crew was happy.

And now she was growing a child with the man she loved, just like she'd always dreamed.

She'd thought she would wander through life lonely, but a chance meeting with a man in a diner had set her destiny on a completely different path. Now, no matter what happened from here on, she wouldn't face this world alone.

Happiness—true, consuming happiness—had existed all this time up here in Damon's mountains. She'd just had to believe in a little magic to find it.

Want More of the Boarlanders?

The Complete Series is Available Now

Other books in this series:

Boarlander Boss Bear
(Boarlander Bears, Book 1)

Boarlander Silverback
(Boarlander Bears, Book 3)

Boarlander Beast Boar
(Boarlander Bears, Book 4)

Boarlander Cursed Boar
(Boarlander Bears, Book 5)

About the Author

T.S. Joyce is devoted to bringing hot shifter romances to readers. Hungry alpha males are her calling card, and the wilder the men, the more she'll make them pour their hearts out. She werebear swears there'll be no swooning heroines in her books. It takes tough-as-nails women to handle her shifters.

Experienced at handling an alpha male of her own, she lives in a tiny town, outside of a tiny city, and devotes her life to writing big stories. Foodie, wolf whisperer, ninja, thief of tiny bottles of awesome smelling hotel shampoo, nap connoisseur, movie fanatic, and zombie slayer, and most of this bio is true.

Bear Shifters? Check
Smoldering Alpha Hotness? Double Check
Sexy Scenes? Fasten up your girdles, ladies and gents, it's gonna to be a wild ride.

For more information on T. S. Joyce's work, visit her website at
www.tsjoycewrites.wordpress.com

51280219R00140

Made in the USA
San Bernardino, CA
17 July 2017